THE KINGS IN
WINTER

THE KINGS IN WINTER

Cecelia Holland

Atheneum   New York

1968

COPY: Y

FOR DAVID JACKSON
who started it all

———————◆———————

Note

In 999, the King of Munster, Brian Boru, trapped an army of Danish invaders and Irish rebels in the defile of Glenmama and massacred them. The leader of the defeated Irish was Maelmordha, the King of Leinster; Leinster and Munster were hereditary enemies and the Danes had marched on Brian at Maelmordha's invitation. Maelmordha himself escaped death at Glenmama by hiding in a yew tree, from which he was personally dragged by King Brian's eldest son Murchad. According to the chroniclers it was Maelmordha's fault that the Danes were trapped.

After his victory, Brian's prestige and power were such that he could successfully claim the Kingship of all Ireland. Traditionally, the High King of Ireland was the head of either of the two branches of the ó Niall family, and in 999 that happened to be Maelsechlainn, King of Tara. Maelsechlainn surrendered the High Seat to Brian but remained a powerful and an important figure. To be the High King was never to command all Ireland: in the end Brian could rely only on his own clan, the Dal gCais.

Maelmordha remained King of Leinster. In token of the truce between Leinster and Munster, King Brian married Maelmordha's sister, Gormflaith. She had already been married to the Danish King of Dublin, and her son by him, Sygtrygg Silkbeard, was now King of that city, and for a while Gormflaith had been Maelsechlainn's wife. Her marriage to Brian lasted only long enough for her to conceive a tremendous hatred for him.

Some years after Brian became High King—in 1011 or so—Maelmordha brought him some tribute—pine trees for the masts of ships. On the way from Leinster to Brian's hall at Kincora, Maelmordha helped carry the trees and popped a button from his shirt. When he got to the hall he took the shirt to Gormflaith to have her mend it. Instead, she threw it into the fire and rebuked him for serving a King of Munster.

To this Maelmordha apparently said nothing untoward. The next day, however, he came on Murchad, the King's son, playing chess, and he told Murchad to make a certain move. Murchad did so and lost the game.

"It was you that gave advice to the Danes when they were defeated," Murchad said.

"I shall give them advice again," Maelmordha said, "and they will not be defeated."

"Have the yew tree made ready for you, then," Murchad said.

At this, Maelmordha stormed out of Kincora. King Brian sent a messenger after him. When the messenger caught up with Maelmordha, Maelmordha struck him so hard on the head that the man's skull fractured.

In the war that followed, King Brian had everything his own way. He was already old, but his energy and his influence would have adorned a man in the prime of his life. And Maelsechlainn helped him. For a year or so, Maelsechlainn and Brian harried the rebels—Maelmordha and his allies, among them the ó Ruairc of Brefni—all across Ireland. The Danes, who lived in their cities on the coasts, helped both sides.

Finally Maelmordha asked the help of his nephew, Sygtrygg the King of Dublin, and here the shape of events changed abruptly. Maelmordha's appeal for help brought to his support not only the Danes of Ireland but Vikings and fighting men from all over the northern seas: "the Foreigners of the Western World," the chronicler calls them. Greatest among them were Sigurd, Jarl of the Orkneys, and Brodir, a renegade whose home port was the Isle of Man. This was no longer a rebellion; this was an invasion. And at his Yule feast, in our year 1013, Jarl Sigurd made it clear that the expedition was not merely to pillage, but to seize and hold all Ireland.

The Danes were summoned to Dublin, to gather by Easter of our year 1014. King Brian heard of it and called all his men to meet near Dublin by Palm Sunday.

This is the historical background for this story. Muirtagh himself, his family and his feud are my inventions.

Cecelia Holland

THE KINGS IN WINTER

SEAT OF THE
ó RUAIRC

SEAT OF THE
MACMAHON

THE
DANISH
KINGDOM
OF
DUBLIN

N

0   50   75   100
MILES

ULSTER

Lough
Neagh

CONNAUGHT

MEATH

Tara

Clontarf
Dublin

Where
Muirtagh
spent the
midwinter

RIVER SHANNON

The stronghold
of the
ó Cullinane

R. LIFFEY

Sliabh
Blum

St. Kevin's
Church

Lough Derg

Kincora

Limerick

LEINSTER

MUNSTER

IRELAND – ca 1014

Morgan

Muirtagh reined in. One of his outriders was galloping down, waving one arm over his head in the signal that meant a large armed force was moving toward them. When he saw that Muirtagh was watching, the outrider pointed back, over the long steep ridge before them.

Cearbhall was beside Muirtagh; he shaded his eyes to see the outrider and pointing to the ridge said, "Let's at least take that hill—then we can hold them off if they should be Danes."

Muirtagh looked back at his men, all standing still, resting. "The hill behind us is closer."

"Why go back when we can go forward?"

"Why run up to meet them?"

Cearbhall frowned. Muirtagh wheeled his pony and trotted back toward his men. "Go back to the crest of this slope and line up, in case they are Danes coming."

His men rose and jogged up the rise, their packbags jouncing on their shoulders. The cattle had just crossed the top of the hill, and at Muirtagh's signal the drovers slowed and stopped them. Muirtagh glanced quickly over his shoulder. The first outrider was almost on him, and the other two were racing in, waving their arms. Hauling the pony's head around, Muirtagh trotted along the line of his men and around the cattle.

The outriders caught up with him, Liam first. "Many of them. All mounted—they look Irish, and they carry the High King's sign."

"We'll wait here. Where is my brother?"

"Here." Cearbhall wedged his tall horse between Liam's and Muirtagh's ponies. "Irish, so close to the Danes' country?"

"Pfft. It's not a wasteland. Liam, go to the end of the

line and watch for my signal."

When the strangers topped the long hill before them, Muirtagh and his men were safely gathered up almost directly across the wide glen. Muirtagh congratulated himself mildly. The other band was larger than his own, but they wouldn't attack so high and ready a point. He slid down from the pony and strung his bow. Behind him, Cearbhall waited, calmly, with his sword across his horse's withers. One of the strangers, on a fine white-faced bay pony, cantered toward them, one hand raised. Muirtagh chose one of his long, owl-fletched arrows and set it to the string.

"Stop there," he said.

"I am Kier mac Aodha," the advance rider said. "Can't you read my device?"

"So near Dublin, nobody reads," Muirtagh said. He put the tip of his bow to the ground. "Come up."

Kier mac Aodha trotted up, keeping a tight hold on his pony. He looked at Muirtagh and at Cearbhall, who was sitting quietly on his horse behind Muirtagh, his great head lifted and his eyes steady. Kier was a young man; he looked puzzled. He said, "I am seeking The ó Cullinane," with a question in the name.

"Here," Muirtagh said. "Muirtagh the Bowman. This is my brother, Cearbhall."

"Cearbhall the Danekiller," Kier said. "Yes." He bowed stiffly to both of them. "In God's name, greeting from the King. He heard that you had come down plundering, and he sent me and my troop to see that you'd come to no bad end."

Muirtagh laughed. He unstrung his bow and sheathed it, and vaulted up onto his pony's back. "Oh, we shall all come to a bad end, sooner or later. We met the Danes we were hunting just south of Dublin, and they came to their bad end sooner than they had expected, I think.

Surely your messages from the King come to more than that?"

The boy licked his lips, swung suddenly to look east, and said, "We should move out, in case you left anyone alive back there to tell which way you'd gone."

Muirtagh signaled to Liam. His men broke out of their line, moving quickly and quietly, gathering into groups and herding the cattle forward. The three horses they'd recovered from the Danes trotted up on leadropes. Muirtagh hung back until the last of the men and cattle had reached the foot of the hill. Kier mac Aodha was waiting. They started off to meet Kier's escort.

Cearbhall rode in close to Muirtagh. "It's odd indeed when a cutting off the tree can turn out as strong a force as a clan chief."

"Not when the clan's ó Cullinane." Muirtagh looked around at the band coming after him, at their well-ordered groups. "It's only God's grace there are so many. Twenty years ago . . ."

He crossed himself. In twenty years his clan hadn't stirred out of their own hills, and now, the first time they marched out, it had brought the High King down on them. He'd been too fond of the success of the raid.

"How many Danes did you fight?" Kier said.

Cearbhall scratched the side of his nose. "As many as we are, half as many more."

The young man's brows jerked up. "You buried your dead in Danish ground?"

Muirtagh stared at the boy's fine tunic. "We didn't lose a man."

"You're to be praised for your valor. Here is a good tale, I'm sure."

"There was no valor," Muirtagh said quickly. "We circled them in the night and charged down like a herd of wild cattle. It was their stupidity for camping in the open, but they thought they were safe."

"Your brother's modest," Kier said to Cearbhall.

Cearbhall leaned forward a little, smiling. "My brother, as his name says, is a bowman, not a warrior. He stands on a hill with his bow, and tells us what to do, and watches us to see that we do it, and if anybody attacks him, he shoots him very coldly with an arrow."

"Had he done so, Cuchulain had died old," Muirtagh said.

"My cousin, the King—" Kier started.

Muirtagh drove a sharp elbow into Cearbhall's ribs. "There, that explains the escort and the pretty shirt. I could have told you there was an explanation. Yes?" He turned and beamed at Kier.

Kier flushed crimson. "My cousin asked if I would escort you to Cathair-by-Tara. He and Maelsechlainn are there, to talk of things touching the Danes, and since your clan lies so near the Danes' kingdom he thought it proper you should join him."

"Maelsechlainn," Muirtagh said. He twisted to sweep his glance over the horizon. The name, even in his own mouth, frightened him a little. He reined in suddenly, so that everybody else had to stop and there was a tangle of kicking horses.

"Liam," he said, "you and the others might as easily go home from here. We'll have no use for a pack of cattle." He paused a moment, his eyes thoughtfully on Cearbhall. "They'll serve us, by Tara, like Tara's King himself." He smiled at Cearbhall.

"Oh, surely—" Kier said, and bit off the words. Muirtagh's band was already moving off, settling into the quick, loose step of hill people. Muirtagh nudged his pony, and to Kier's obvious surprise they were off again, the horsemen starting up with a jerk as if Muirtagh, small in their midst, drew on the reins.

Cearbhall's deep voice said, "Maelsechlainn, King's cousin, is an old ally of The mac Mahon, and The mac Mahon and The ó Cullinane have in the past come to blows, a bit."

Muirtagh knew that Cearbhall would be looking at him; he stared at Kier's fine tunic. "It ended my father, it ruined my clan, and Maelsechlainn had no small part in that."

"Surely my cousin knows of this feud," Kier said. "It's hard to believe the High King would draw blood enemies together."

Twenty years before Maelsechlainn had been the High King. And he had drawn them together.

"My brother distrusts the world," Cearbhall was saying. "He trusts too much in God to like the ordinary run of us. But when you get to know him, you can grow quite fond of him." He palmed Muirtagh's shoulder. "Speak sweetly to this gentleman, Muirtagh."

"You must pardon me, sir," Muirtagh said, "if I'm abrupt or rough in my speech, but I am a poor man and haven't had your advantages of birth."

He crowded his pony against Cearbhall's horse and said quietly, "Remember who is the chief here. I'm little enough without your cutting at me."

Cearbhall looked surprised. Muirtagh pulled off a little, knowing that Cearbhall would never stay quiet.

"Is mac Laig at Cathair?" Cearbhall said.

"I believe so," Kier said.

"There. That should soothe you." To Kier he said, "He's mad for harpers. Any wanderer in Ireland, if his harp has only one string and he whistles when he sings, has a dish at our table, and Muirtagh discourses with him very weightily on matters of poesy."

Muirtagh shut his eyes a moment, resigned. "It keeps my stringfingers tuned," he said, plucking at the bowcase beside his knee.

They went on a little way. Finally Kier said, "It's rare that one sees a man with a bow, these days."

Muirtagh looked all around again, searching the horizon. "How would you suggest a man my size should fight a man as big as my brother? Blade to blade?"

"It's the honorable way," Kier said.

Muirtagh looked at him; the boy was slender, not much taller than Muirtagh himself, and neat in his good clothes, like a bit of jewelry. "Oh, well," he said gently, "there are men who could, but I'm not one. I have more important things to worry about."

They rode on. Kier said, "What?"

Muirtagh looked at him. "What what?"

Cearbhall laughed, shaking his head.

Muirtagh rolled Maelsechlainn's name around in his mind—the subtlest King since Conchubar. Maelsechlainn had a wonderful memory and could forget when that served his purpose. Now the King of Munster was the High King, and Muirtagh thought that Maelsechlainn had forgotten some certain things.

"Who else will be at Cathair?"

Kier turned toward him. "The chiefs of all the great clans of Meath—"

"The mac Mahon."

"Well, yes. And some Ulstermen. Many of them were already there when I rode out. The hall will be packed full."

"Which of Ulster?" Cearbhall said, and he and Kier discussed the chiefs. Muirtagh glanced at the horizon. It was an old game, and he'd been long out of it, hiding shyly up in his hills: the gathering of the clans, setting the chiefs together and drawing them separate, the High King weaving all their loyalties into his cloak.

Walk the middle of them, he thought, and smile, and

bow, and speak as softly as Cearbhall will let me. The
mac Mahon may go and cut his own throat and blame
that on me. Twenty years long? Perhaps he's forgotten
too. It isn't he, it's his son, one of his sons. The third was
his Tanist, I think. The old man died in his bed, cursing
God. They might have told me that to placate me.

Cearbhall had heard that news and moaned that now
he might not kill the old man. Even then, before he was
big enough to keep the hem of his tunic out of the dust,
Cearbhall had moaned. And gone off, as soon as their father's swordbelt fit him, gone off with their mother
screeching behind him, leaving the fields and the herds
and the people to Muirtagh, gone off with his eyes bright
from staring into fires while the tales were told.

Now, on his lean downcountry horse, Cearbhall talked
to the High King's cousin in his measured voice—no
boy, so different from the little thing that had followed
Muirtagh, crying out to him to wait, and still the same, so
much that now and again Muirtagh wanted to laugh at
the pleasure of having his own brother back. Even with
Cearbhall tugging at him, pulling at him to go down, to
go back, to get their revenge.

"They'd stolen a herd of our cattle and three of our
best horses," Cearbhall said to Kier, speaking of the raid.
"So we went after them to get the herds back. That was
all. They weren't Sygtrygg's men, and anyhow, Sygtrygg's not in Dublin now."

They'd heard news of Cearbhall, of course, even back
in the hills—so close to Kevin's Church they saw many
travelers. Old Finnlaith, Muirtagh's mother's father, at
first had asked any stranger who passed through for
news of Cearbhall, but he'd grown weary of that later.

"He's the same as all the rest," the old man had said.
"Maybe he'll never come back home."

Muirtagh had been going out the door, and he'd

turned, surprised. The old man had been a fighter in his day, and even now stood taller and heavier than many young men.

"He'll come home," Muirtagh had answered. "When we go down again."

"Hah," the old man had said. "Since they hoisted you up and made you chief they've poked and prodded at you to lead them down again. I'd rather stay up here, where at least we can see if anyone's coming to kill us. Where are you going?"

"To bring the cattle in."

The old man had snorted. "In the plain, just to talk of fighting they'll let the cattle wander to the sea."

Cearbhall said, "Praying, brother?"

Muirtagh looked around at him. "Sunk in prayer out of sight."

He began to sing, and immediately everyone else joined in. They sang all the way to Cathair.

When they reached the fort it was already past sundown. The great stockade lay in the valley some little distance from Tara of the Kings, in among the fields and pastureland; it was neat and trim like all Maelsechlainn's doings. Sentries let them through the gate, and attendants swarmed around them to take their horses and ponies, to bring them water to wash in and cloth to dry their hands, fine linen. To Kier the servants bowed and gave immediate deference. They smelled the mountains on Muirtagh and Cearbhall and weren't so soft with them.

The dark gable of the hall rose above them. Muirtagh could hear, inside, the loud voices and clank of metal, and he folded his arms around him. With attendants at their heels and hands they flooded through the door and into the dim torchlight.

There, in the High Seat, the High King sat, and beside him Maelsechlainn, wreathed in smoky torchlight. The smell of food was like a blow. A herald bellowed their names into the chatter of voices. Above the tables leading down from the High Seat to the door, the mobbed faces turned like hogs' snouts to see who was coming in to share the food.

Beside him, Cearbhall stiffened, and Muirtagh caught his arm at the wrist and looked where he was looking and saw a mac Mahon. By his clothes he was the chief, and he was watching them, his head down.

"Let it go," Muirtagh said, and started forward. He moved fast, breaking out of the group of servants before any could attend him, and he pulled all eyes to him. He walked straight to the High Seat and bowed.

The High King was even older than his grandfather, bent and rutted with the weight of age, his long beard and hair dead white. Under the sparse pale brows, his eyes were faded. Beside him Maelsechlainn with his snowy beard and small, smiling mouth seemed hardly out of youth.

"Muirtagh," the High King said. "So, Aed's son, you are."

His voice was deeper than Muirtagh remembered, the melody harsher. Maelsechlainn could sit and smile all he wished; he'd not have his High Seat back from this one.

"Lord," Muirtagh said, "Aed's son, and The ó Cullinane."

The old man shifted a little, one elbow awkwardly bent. "It's pleasant to have old names again in my court. Your brother I know." He nodded at Cearbhall. Muirtagh glanced back, startled that Cearbhall had followed him.

"Cearbhall is my Tanist," Muirtagh said.

"I'm pleased you went back to your clan, Danekiller," the High King said, "although we have more work for you on the coasts."

Cearbhall made some gesture. His ears were red. Muirtagh looked at Maelsechlainn and found the King of
Tara's dark eyes on him.

"I remember a rather small boy," Maelsechlainn said—
his voice grated, from long memory and the fresh hearing; it was a mealy, delighted voice. "Now I see a rather
small man."

"Ah," Muirtagh said. "But you haven't changed."

He knew he'd think of some reply, too late, that
would have curdled Maelsechlainn. The High King was
choosing attendants for them, to escort them to a bench.
He directed them to a place of honor on the right side.
The mac Mahon sat on the left among his followers. In
the shuffle, Muirtagh looked up and saw Maelsechlainn's
eyes on him, the small mouth smiling, the long fingers
twining in his beard. They sat.

Immediately they were served, roast pork, venison,
beef, salmon and other fish, and wine poured into their
cups. Kier mac Aodha was sitting at the High King's side,
picking bits from his plate. Around them, as if the hall
had swallowed them up, the low mumble of conversation
began again.

Muirtagh, looking around him, remembered faces,
placed new ones. He looked at the gross slab of meat on
his dish, made the sign of the Cross over it, and picked up
his knife to cut it. The man beside him wheeled heavily
and said, "Is this a monk, this chief?"

Cearbhall tensed, and Muirtagh jabbed him in the ribs
with one elbow. He smiled at the big man. "I find it at
least as good as unicorn's horn," he said. "The meat we
have in Ireland these days one can only trust in God."

"Are you afraid of being poisoned?" the man bawled.
Immediately half the table stopped talking to listen.

"Only by the venom of my own tongue," Muirtagh
said. "In God's name, if Christ could turn water to wine

at Cana, a sinner like me could turn good meat to bad at Cathair."

The man looked suspicious—he had a heavy-jowled face like a bullock's. Muirtagh put down his knife and signed the Cross over the big man's meat. "A false priest may baptize, isn't that so?"

Somebody somewhere laughed. The big man scowled. "I can't follow what you're saying."

"All the better for me. A deer untracked isn't killed. A poor hunter you must be if a word that only circles in front of your nose eludes you. Now, eat your meat; sinners' blessings don't last long."

Now all the men around were laughing, and, not to be left out, the ones who couldn't have heard joined in. Muirtagh devoted himself to eating. The big man beside him settled back, muttered, and took a bite of his food. Cearbhall laughed softly, his mouth full of meat.

When the beef was eaten, someone brought mutton and filled up Muirtagh's winecup again. Cearbhall worked his way steadily through what seemed to Muirtagh whole cows and sheep and great lakes of wine. All of them did. When Muirtagh sat back, finished, they went on eating, and most of them had been eating before he and Cearbhall came. The High King, alone of them all, hadn't touched his dinner.

Now and then some of them would stand up and leave the hall, but when they came back they fell to eating as if the walk outside and back had famished them.

Muirtagh waved off the attendant with the wine ewer, saw the man's shocked face, and smiled. He let his eyes wander down the table toward The mac Mahon and his men. They were all eating, their great forearms lying comfortably on the table. Big, they were, and strong, like Cearbhall, maybe showing the Danish blood; but they were all black-haired. Black as Muirtagh's. He sat quietly, watching and listening, like a bit of millet between the two grindstones of the big men on either side.

The attendants rushed back and forth, carrying the platters and ewers, their heels clacking on the floor. A harper came in, sat down at the High King's foot, and began to play. Muirtagh's ears stretched. After a few notes, he settled back, his eyes drifting around the tables. This was not mac Laig.

The harper played some passable verses, sang decently, and discreetly left. The High King sat askew in his chair, his old fingers tapping at the carved arm. Now and then he spoke to Kier mac Aodha. The feasting began to lag. Here and there a man rose, stretched, and wandered outside, returning to sit talking to a neighbor. The trenchers vanished in the hands of the servants. Maelsechlainn called to one of his friends from Meath and they discussed some detail of a hunt they'd both been on, across half the length of the hall and in high voices. Muirtagh watched Maelsechlainn's face. The presence of the High King reassured him; he realized, suddenly, that he wasn't afraid of Maelsechlainn.

One of The mac Mahon's men looked up, looked past Muirtagh to Cearbhall, and measured him narrowly. Muirtagh nudged his brother. Cearbhall lifted his great head and stared, his eyes unblinking, down at the other man. Shortly they looked away, as if by common signal, and Cearbhall called for more wine.

Nearby, a man with an Ulster accent mentioned Maelmordha, and the name sped around the hall. Someone laughed and shook his head. Maelsechlainn frowned; Maelmordha he had always hated, of course. Muirtagh shrugged, mentally. Maelsechlainn said the name—Muirtagh saw his lips move—and turned his head to stare at Muirtagh. Muirtagh made the sign against the Evil Eye and laughed in the King of Tara's face.

"They tell me you're a harper," the High King said. He spoke above the casual roar of the others' speech, but at the sound of his voice they all grew quiet. "I'd thought all Gaels described themselves as either poet or warrior, but never both."

Muirtagh got to his feet. "Some are neither, sir, as you must know well. My brother here's the warrior—we only permit one, in my father's sons. Poet I am not, but if it would please you, I could perhaps strum a little."

The old man looked from side to side. "I remember the ó Cullinanes as quick-fingered men. Fetch him a harp."

Cearbhall plucked at Muirtagh's sleeve, drew him down, and whispered, "This is Maelsechlainn's doing."

"Pfft. It's only the dapper little King's cousin who didn't like the way I looked at his gold-stitched tunic." Muirtagh swung up to sit on the table, his legs dangling over the edge, and took the harp. He balanced it, rocked it back and forth a little until it seated itself, and ran his fingers over the strings once, tentatively.

"Quicker-fingered with a bow," he said. He played a little jig, watching the harp strings shimmer. There was no reason to look elsewhere; they were all watching him. He played the opening stave of the Cuchulain tale, rambled through that a little, and switched abruptly into the jig again. He took a deep breath, steadying himself.

"My father's ollumh taught me the art," he said. "In the hills. He needed someone to teach, poor thing, because he hadn't died when he thought he should have." He played part of an old lament. "He chose me for lack of more suitable material."

He stopped playing and took the ring from his right arm. Cearbhall reached out to take it. Muirtagh shifted a little. They were quiet, all around. Oh, God, yes. They were quiet.

"As you know," he said, playing the jig again, "all of

you, acute men that you are, there are few left to my clan. There were fewer still, when I was first the chief, due to a certain matter of which we may not speak here." He looked up at the roof. "It's dead and gone, God save it." His fingers on the strings parodied the rhythm of his voice.

He looked up and around the room, smiling at them all, his lips stiff. His back was aching, deep by his spine. His eyes stayed longest on Tara's King, up there at the end of the hall. He looked back at the harp.

"Hill songs are different from plain songs. Here's one. My father might have taught me the songs of Meath, but the ollumh would not, and my father died, oh, twenty years ago, as you all know."

As you all know, the harp sang. It slid easily into the part of Dierdre's song where she warns the sons of Usnech not to go back to Ireland. The mac Mahon was sitting unnaturally straight, down there among all his kindred.

"We needn't speak of it," Muirtagh said. "If it should fret you."

He hummed through the song and broke into the jig again.

"Do you sing?" the old King asked.

"No, lord. I harp."

He played the most intricate of the tales of Cuchulain to prove that. His heart galloped in his throat, like the chariot in the song. Halfway through it he picked up the jig again, and he saw them all shiver.

"It was King's work, that summer night, such that a humble man like me might not understand." The harp sang gaily under his fingers. "There was something of an oath, I've heard—some grand, full-worded oath sworn under moonlight. I know little of oaths myself, having taken only one."

The jig sped faster and he looked around, his brows arched. "Does no one wish to dance?"

The mac Mahon was staring at the High King, trying to catch his eye, but the High King looked elsewhere.

"Here's a dusty thing to have off the rack now," Muirtagh said. "After twenty years. My brother's never heard it, being of a tender age. But perhaps you may remember it."

The strings thundered out the first phrases of the ó Cullinane war song. The whole hallful of men flinched. The song faltered and slowed and sighed away. Muirtagh shuddered uncontrollably. He looked around at all the white, set faces.

"Nobody played that the night you killed my father. You gave us other music then. Murders, and naked men cut down, and the women slain, and the children slain, and bleeding feet running off into the hills, yes, and being frightened and hungry and cold, but that's all gone now and twenty years would restore Judas to good company in these days. Isn't that so, gentlemen?"

He lifted the harp in both hands and broke it over his knee. The strings screeched.

"But after all," he said, "Christ died for our sins."

He flung the two halves of the harp across the room, swung back across the table, and sat down next to Cearbhall. The crowd of men sat still, in dull silence. Muirtagh put his chin on his chest and shut his eyes.

The silence grew, as if no one could bear to break it, and he felt all his rage ebb away from him. He lifted his head, stretching the muscles of his neck, and said, "You may speak now. You have the permission of a rather small man."

He looked at Maelsechlainn. He was tired, and he wanted to go home, and Maelsechlainn's forced bitter laugh hardly mattered. The hall stirred. Slowly, their voices began to mutter and rise, and the sound grew into a general roar. Cearbhall bent down, his mouth close to Muirtagh's ear, and said, "You've frightened them. They thought perhaps we'd forgotten."

"They never thought that. They thought they'd forgotten. That's the way with them."

Cearbhall shrugged and reached for his winecup.

"I will forgive them," Muirtagh said, "as long as they don't forget."

"Why forgive them at all?"

"It seems easier that way."

He pretended to be interested in the grain of the wood in the table, his shoulder to Cearbhall. He felt his brother's anger like a wave of heat from a fevered man, but Cearbhall said nothing.

Cearbhall belonged here. In this hall, Cearbhall should be The ó Cullinane. Muirtagh felt small and rather mad. That had been a mad thing to do, that thing with the harp, probably foolish. Meaching little pride. He pushed his fingertips together and watched his fingers bend.

A heavy weight slammed against the opposite side of the table, and Muirtagh looked up. A big young red-headed man stood there, ungainly, one hand on the table-top.

"What did that mean?" he said.

Cearbhall was rigid beside Muirtagh, one hand fisted on the table before him. Muirtagh said, "Who are you?"

"Cormac ó Daugherty, Niall's Tanist."

"Go away, then. You might not ask such questions of an anointed chief."

From the looks on the faces of the other men, Cormac had sprung up on impulse, without being bidden to it, and even Cearbhall was leaning back, murmuring to the man on his right. Cormac was standing in that peculiar fashion, half leaning on the table, vivid with rage. Muirtagh put his elbows on the table and his chin in his hands. "Go away," he said mildly.

Cormac went. No one laughed at him, but many men smiled. The man whose meat Muirtagh had blessed turned ponderously and said, "How do you winter, up there in the hills?"

"Oh, we have grass enough, in the glens. The wind's such that I worry for the gable and the thatch, but at least my gate-yard's not a swamp all winter, like some on the plain."

"Last winter there were days we thought we'd lost a child or two in the mud."

"We have plenty of turf."

"Colder, is it. I —"

A herald ran out into the middle of the floor and banged his staff down three times. "Listen, chiefs. Listen, warriors. The High King of Ireland is speaking."

The King stood up before the High Seat and made the sign of the Cross. "God be with us here. We have news of a special sort that needs your counsel."

The conversation was swept away. The old man, still square-shouldered, stood as if he pushed his back up against the weight of years. He looked around him, at each of them, and said, "Here's word from the Outer Islands and from Dublin, both, that Sygtrygg Silkbeard, Gormflaith's son, and the Jarl of the Orkneys are plotting to bring a Danish army here to help Maelmordha, the rebel King of Leinster. We heard it all from a man who was there at Jarl Sigurd's Yuletide."

Muirtagh half shut his eyes, thinking of something he might say to Maelmordha the next time they met.

"The ó Cullinane is a Leinsterman," Maelsechlainn said.

Muirtagh lifted his head. "What King ever laid claim to those hills? He's never come asking me for a tax."

The High King said, "The ó Cullinanes have been Meathmen since the Great Flood. Here's no time to quibble over boundaries." He shot Maelsechlainn a glare, and his eye shone like a jewel in the torchlight. "There's more to this than I've said so far. Sygtrygg and Gormflaith have been calling up all the men they can find, from all the viks and islands—this time they mean to have all Ireland."

All around the hall, chiefs leaned back, muttered, looked up at the ceiling, and pretended to be shrewd and thoughtful. Cearbhall was drawing designs on the table-top with his forefinger, his brows drawn together. Muirtagh thought again of Maelmordha and sighed.

"If you'll give an ear to a man at odds with most of you," Cearbhall said, "we might have thought of this long ago."

His voice was deep and strong as the King's, and when he lifted his head the gesture seemed to cleave the air.

"Over and over again," he said, "we Irish have beaten the Danes." He nodded to the King, almost curtly. "You yourself, lord, threw Sygtrygg once out of Dublin. Never have we shut Ireland to them, they always come back, and they always find welcome."

"They are good traders," someone said.

"So," Cearbhall answered. "They are good traders. First they come with swords and axes, and we rightly turn them off; now they come with goods and money, and we take them in. They have swords and axes in their baggage, and we use them to fight each other with."

"Rebels," the High King said, frowning.

"Such distinctions are for Irish minds," Muirtagh said. "The Danes are less careful about such things."

"Now's the season when we must throw them all out or take them all in," Cearbhall said. "And all, like the stones the wolf ate, would sink us into the sea."

One of The mac Mahon's men jumped up, banged his fist on the table, and said, "God knows there's nothing gentle between me and any son of Aed ó Cullinane's, but Cearbhall is right. Here and now, we have to turn the shield to the sea."

All the men began to leap up and down, clapping and yelling, rattling their weapons, until Muirtagh put his hands over his ears and shut his eyes. Several men were speaking at once, saying nothing more than that they agreed with Cearbhall and each other. Muirtagh lowered his hands and eyed the High King, who was sitting down again and looking steadily from one man to the next.

"Muirtagh," Maelsechlainn said. "Aside from distinctions, what do you say about all this?"

Maelsechlainn had the most marvelous memory in all Ireland. Muirtagh waited a moment, trying to gather himself up. The shouting dimmed a little. He said, "If they come, we must fight them. I think you waste your breath, shouting here."

At that, the shouting doubled. The High King leaned on the arm of his chair and said, smiling, "In this, we aren't so unlike the Danes, Muirtagh."

"We're like a man who knows he has to face a terrible enemy, and puts on all his armor and takes all his weapons in his hands, and steps outside the gate, and finds there facing him another man in all his armor, with all his weapons in his hands."

The High King thought about that, glancing off down the hall, and said, "You're far more troublesome than you think you are."

In all the shouting and stamping a little road of silence ran between the two of them, under their locked eyes. Muirtagh said, "If you want me troublesome, you may be disappointed. I'm not the sort for it."

Suddenly the old man laughed. "You have a bad sense

of drama for a harper. Must you be so commonplace?"

"It's a harper's duty to show the shape of things, lord, not the froth that blows across them and obscures them. Isn't that so?"

"My ollumh, mac Laig, told me once that a harper must show men what they should be." The King had twisted all around to face Muirtagh, and his eyes glowed.

"Exactly, lord. Isn't that what I said?"

"You said one should show things as they are."

Muirtagh laughed. "Ah, well—if the shape of a rock you see in your mind is different from the shape of the rock you see on the shore, who's to say it isn't the difference that's important?"

That wide mouth twitched into a smile. "A pretty point."

The chiefs were rising to leave, and the King turned to look at them. "We have beds for you in the outbuildings, should you wish them."

"You'll forgive us if we go home. It's not so far."

Cearbhall was standing, and Muirtagh rose. The King said, "You will attend me at Kincora soon, I hope. It's near the Lough and we can observe rocks."

"My life's something different from most chiefs—I have an overbearing wife, and she makes me work. But someday."

"Overbearing?" Cearbhall said. "Aud isn't—"

"Come along, brother. We're going home."

"But the others are staying here."

"Well, I'm for home. Stay if you want to, but find me some torches so that I don't lose my way."

"I'll come with you."

They followed the last of the crowd into the courtyard and Muirtagh found a groom to bring his pony and Cearbhall's horse. Cearbhall collected torches and a pot of coals. It was a bright, starry night, a rare night, warmer than usual. While they waited for the horses Cearbhall said, "What was that song you played—the one you said I wouldn't know?"

"Your father's war song."

They mounted and rode out, Cearbhall holding the torch. The night closed down around them, and the torchlight reached only a little way into it. The pony settled into a quick singlefoot. Cearbhall held his horse down to keep even with Muirtagh.

"Do you know your way?" Cearbhall said.

"Yes." Muirtagh looked over his shoulder for the Pole Star and headed straight away from it.

"Do you still not like riding at night?"

Muirtagh shrugged. They were crossing the fat ground of Meath now, plowed and pastured ground. "We'll not reach the hills until dawn," he said. They swerved to pass a stand of beech trees.

Yes. I hate to ride at night. Around him the dark murmured, muttered, wound its fingers toward him. The torchlight wobbled over the ground. Off to the left, a blasted tree made a nearly human shape against the sky. He kept his eyes from it. It was a tree. It was a tree. He sneaked a look through the corner of his eye. The tree's stumps of branches fluttered at him and he crossed himself. He looked again for the Pole Star and corrected their course a little.

"I'm tired," Cearbhall said.

"Go to sleep, then."

Cearbhall handed him the torch and his rein, folded his arms across his chest, and dozed off. Muirtagh hooked the rein over his wrist. He felt suddenly guilty about the harp trick; if they'd been willing to let it rest he thought he should have. Except that it was his to finish it.

There was something behind him.

He resisted the urge to look over his shoulder; his ears

strained. He could hear nothing. A light mist was seeping up out of the ground, muffling the noise even of his own pony's hoofs. The horizon ahead was rumpled with low brush and trees bent against the wind. Behind him something struck clearly through the mist, a sharp cracking sound.

"Cearbhall."

"What?"

"Listen." He slipped the rein from his wrist.

They rode on a little way, dragging the circle of torchlight around them. Suddenly Cearbhall reined in.

Muirtagh stopped a little ahead of him and listened, looking straight ahead. He thought he heard it again. The mist was veiling the stretch of brush ahead of them.

Cearbhall jogged up. "Give me a torch and the coal pot."

Muirtagh handed them over to him. "Get off a little bit and stay still."

He turned the pony and kicked it into a fast trot. Cearbhall faded off out of the torchlight. The mist lay only as high as a man's knees from the ground; off down the plain he saw the rustling edge of the Eastern Wood, clear and black. The pony moved quickly along, his head swaying from side to side, casting shadows in the torchlight.

Hoofbeats sounded close behind him—that must be Cearbhall. Below the loud clatter he heard other hoofs, three or four sets. He reined in and whirled the pony. Cearbhall galloped up.

"Three?" Muirtagh said.

"Yes." The hoofbeats beyond them had stopped. "Human, at least."

Muirtagh couldn't see if he was smiling. "There's a steep rise up ahead. We'll ride to go past it and lead them under, and swing back to get above them."

The mist was rising higher. Muirtagh started off, holding the pony down to a slower pace. The steep hill's dim outline appeared before them, slowly heaving up out of the grassland. Cearbhall was uneasy, twitching, his hand on his swordhilt. Muirtagh rode close to the foot of the slope. He could hear the horses behind them coming on, catching up now.

They reached the far side of the hill and Muirtagh wheeled the pony, driving him up the slope. The pony leaned hard to keep his balance, snorting with each stride, and behind him Cearbhall's horse slipped and staggered and lunged after. Halfway up the hill Muirtagh leapt down, strung his bow, and called out, "Who's there?"

The three horsemen below were confused. They stopped moving, muddled about a little, and slowly started off the way they'd come. Muirtagh looked quickly for Cearbhall, didn't see him, and shouted, "Stand where you are—I can see you."

One of the horsemen down there tried to charge him, but the slope was too steep and his horse refused it. Muirtagh shot the horse.

"In God's name," Kier mac Aodha's voice cried. "Why do you shoot at us? We only came to ask you something."

"Who else?"

"Cormac ó Daugherty and Shane mac Mahon."

"And the King took such care to sit us across from The mac Mahon, but he sends one of them after us to give us some little message?" He looked for Cearbhall in the mist. "What is it, some summons to a christening?"

"The King sent to find out why you left so soon."

"Go tell him that something one of you said set me to thinking, and I do my best thinking in my own house, with my wife there to listen to me talk to myself."

He was moving, slowly, through the mist toward Kier's voice. His skin prickled up. The grass was slick with the mist.

"Then there's no reason—" Kier began.

Off to Muirtagh's left something collided with something else, and Cearbhall called out, "Kier mac Aodha, which of your friends have I got here?"

"Oh, God," Kier said.

"That I doubt," Muirtagh said. "Cearbhall?"

"Kier's where you hear him, another behind him, and the third I've got."

"You haven't killed him, have you?" Kier shouted.

Muirtagh scurried down to the foot of the slope, picked out two shapes, and nocked an arrow.

"No," Cearbhall said, answering Kier.

"Don't move," Muirtagh said. "Cearbhall, go fetch their horses."

"Maybe I will kill him," Cearbhall said thoughtfully.

"Get the horses, child. We haven't the time."

Cearbhall moved. Muirtagh, watching the two men below him, ran over to where his pony was waiting and scrambled onto the broad back. Cearbhall and two horses cantered off, away from Kier and the others.

"King's cousin," Muirtagh called, "if anyone asks after your fine horses, send to me, and I will have them back to you. God be with you all, gentlemen."

He galloped down to meet Cearbhall, and they rode quickly away. Once they were far from the hill they settled down into a jog again.

"Well," Muirtagh said. "Here we are, two horses richer." The two were good horses, also, not ponies.

"He'll send for them."

"He won't dare tell the King he came after us. Three men, and not a chief among them—what's Ireland coming to?" He lit a fresh torch. "Now let's go home."

They crossed through the Danes' country just before dawn and rode into the hills. Muirtagh's pony and Cearbhall's horse tired, and they changed to the two new horses. At noon they stopped and rested, eating bread and dried beef Muirtagh had in his packs, and by midafternoon they were above Kevin's Church, in the Glen of the Two Lakes. They turned west and rode over the high, rolling ground where the monks cut their turf. In the middle of the afternoon, they jogged past the first cairn that marked the edge of the clan's country and angled down the slope to the glen where the ó Cullinanes had their stronghold.

All the cattle were in the upper end of the long glen, below the sheer cliff and the waterfall; only a few sheep cropped the grass they rode over. After they crossed the river they saw the stockade, and from the waving and shouting of the sentry, he had seen them. Muirtagh looked beyond the stockade at the waterfall, like a patch of snow between the two brown arches of the hills. He'd loved it since the first time he'd seen it.

"There's Aud," Cearbhall said.

Two people were waiting by the open gate of the stockade. Muirtagh kicked up his horse.

"I still don't see why you think she's overbearing," Cearbhall said.

"Oh, it was a joke. Don't tell her that."

Outside the gate they dismounted and a man came out to take the horses. Aud walked forward, smiling, her skirt whipping around her ankles in the wind.

"You came home richer than one would have thought," she said. "And naturally in time to sit down to dinner with us. Hello, Cearbhall."

"Father."

Four small heads thrust out the gate, turned their bright eyes on Muirtagh, and charged.

"Deliver me," Muirtagh said. "Aud—"

The four children, yelping, swarmed over him. They attached themselves to his arms, belt and back, climbed up him like a tree, and pummeled him madly. Aud laughed. She took Cearbhall by the sleeve and led him into the yard, and Muirtagh, making sure all his children were clinging firmly, gathered up the littlest like a skirt and followed.

In the wide yard most of the people had come out to see them home, and they shouted and waved. Eoghan, Muirtagh's eldest son, began to sing a marching song, keeping time on Muirtagh's shoulders.

"Aren't you a bit old for that?" Muirtagh yelled at him, and shoved through the door into his house.

"Not quite yet," Eoghan said.

Muirtagh stopped in the middle of the floor and shed them. Aud had given Cearbhall a cup of something to drink. "What's for dinner?" he asked her.

"If it's boiled beef I'm back to Tara," Muirtagh said. Eoghan was dismounted at last and behaving like a nearly grown boy, but Aoir was swinging on his arm and screaming.

"Look at me, Father. Father, look."

He looked down at her. "Now, you look no different than when I left."

All of them roared with laughter. Eoghan and Niall dragged him toward a bench and made him sit down, and the two youngest burrowed into his lap. He held Aoir firmly down with one hand and said, over her head, "Nothing happened while I was gone?"

"Nothing untoward." Aud was pouring usquebaugh into a cup. Her wide calm eyes studied him. "Where did you get the two horses?"

"We traded for them." Conall, the littlest, began to jump up and down on Muirtagh's knee. "One dead horse for the two, and they're good ones, and the dead one wasn't even ours. . . . Conall, sit down."

Aud put the cup down in front of Muirtagh and expertly peeled the children off. "And not a man killed. The women are all praising your name."

"I swear," Cearbhall said, "it was the dullest raid I've ever been on."

At the sound of his voice the children all stopped scrambling about and went to stand behind Muirtagh's chair. When Aud went by Conall clutched at her skirts with both hands and walked along beside her. Muirtagh drank nearly half the usquebaugh in one gulp and set it down again.

Eoghan said, "Father, did you bring me a sword?"

"Did I bring you a sword? What do you mean, did I bring you a sword?"

Eoghan's expression was desperate. "You promised you'd bring me a sword."

"Oh. Did I?" He looked at Aud.

"There was mention of it." She retrieved Cearbhall's cup and filled it again. A pair of her women came in and and began arranging the pots for the dinner.

"I forgot," Muirtagh said to Eoghan. "You have your wooden sword, play with that."

"Oh, Father, you forgot?"

"I'm sorry. You aren't old enough, anyway."

"God's blood," Cearbhall said. "You'll have the boy in a long shirt the rest of his life. He's old as I was when I got my first sword. Older. And bigger."

"Father—"

"No. Go outside."

"Father, please."

"I said go outside."

Eoghan muttered, turned away, and marched through the door. Niall and Aoir followed, looking back reproachfully at Muirtagh.

"Don't interfere with me and my children," Muirtagh said to Cearbhall.

"You promised," Aud said. "Are you done with that?"

"No. I don't remem—"

"I have an old sword the boy can have," Cearbhall said.

"He'd have the heads off all the ponies in a week."

"Ssssh," Aud said. "Finnlaith's asleep. It's boiled mutton, by the way."

"Give him something more to drink," Cearbhall said. "He's been touchy ever since Tara."

"What took you there, anyway?" she said. She sat down, keeping one eye on the serving women.

"The High King had in mind to tell us all how the world's to end."

"Oh? Are the women to be there, or is it for the men only, this time?"

Cearbhall said, "How old is Eoghan?"

Aud looked surprised. "Why, he was born the winter after we came here to live."

Muirtagh stiffened, knowing what Cearbhall would say, and Cearbhall said, "He's as old as you were when you were named the chief. He—"

"Stop dabbling your fingers in my children's lives. Dear God, he's only eight—is it even eight?—years younger than you. You're closer to him than you are to me. You—"

"You're going to wake Finnlaith," Aud said. "Cearbhall, go out and call in the men, will you?"

Cearbhall got up, and Aud managed to stay between him and Muirtagh, leaning across Muirtagh to get his cup, until Cearbhall was out the door. Muirtagh said,

"Have I ever told you you—"

"Many times. Don't get angry, you look so funny when you're angry. I'd have thought you'd learned to smile back at him by now."

"Yap yap yap."

"Oh, stop acting like such a child. The old man's something sick, by the way."

"Has he been out of the loft?"

She shook her head. "I've fed him there. Will you take it up to him? I almost fell, the last time."

"What's there to take?"

"Some bread and broth. Here." She went to the fire and dipped broth out of the cauldron. Muirtagh followed her. Her hair, bound neatly into the gold rings, hung down her back, and he pulled it gently.

"I'm sorry."

"You're tired. You can't sleep properly on a horse. Here."

He took the bowl with a napkin over it and went outside. The last light was dribbling out of the yard. Eoghan and Niall ran past him at their mother's shout. Muirtagh climbed up the uneven stair to the loft, juggling the bowl.

The old man was lying in the great bed, right under the eaves, with a deerhound curled up at his feet. He pushed himself up on his elbows and said, "Now, that isn't Aud."

"It's me, Grandfather."

"Oh. When did you get back? Nobody ever tells me anything. Liam said you had the Danes like deer. Ah." He sniffed at the broth.

"Oh, well, I'm not a man to bang a sword on a shield and call it deep speech. Aud says you aren't coming out of bed these days."

"I knew when Cearbhall came back I should fade.

There's something about him I dislike."

"He's an honest man, and there are moments when he's clever. He spoke up in front of the High King, and if what he said wasn't new, at least he used the words well. He's not afraid of the things I am, either."

"He's fey."

Muirtagh frowned. "Pfft. He's got Aed's head on his shoulders. You just think he's Aed."

The old man braced himself and blew on the broth to cool it. He dipped in a chunk of bread. "Just keep him away from The mac Mahon. Will there be a war?"

"Oh, maybe. You know how they talk—all their resolution goes up in words, like smoke."

"Muirtagh," Aud's voice called, down in the yard.

"Send up Eoghan," the old man said. "I'd rather he slept here than Niall. Niall kicks. And Conall's worse."

"I will. Shall I open the window shutter?"

"No. The light bothers me."

"Muirtagh?"

"I'm coming," he shouted. Softer, he said to Finnlaith, "Goodnight. I'll talk to you tomorrow."

He went down the stair and out into the yard. She was standing by the hall door, so that the light limned her. He started slowly across the yard, bending down now and then to pick up a stone and throw it over the stockade fence. She smiled at him and went ahead of him into the hall, where his people were gathered at the table. He shut the door after him.

After they'd eaten, Aud put Conall, Aoir and Niall to bed in the smaller of the two sleeping rooms, brought out the baby and fed him, sitting by the fire. The men of Muirtagh's house got up to go out to the small bed-houses, talking and yawning. Cearbhall cleaned his gear.

"What do you think of Finnlaith?" Aud asked.

Eoghan came over and stood hanging on the back of Muirtagh's chair, his arms around Muirtagh's neck. Muirtagh said, "He's too old, I suppose. His hands are cold."

"That's how it is with old men," Cearbhall said. "What will we do for the war?"

"War?" Aud and Eoghan said together.

"The High King's old, Maelsechlainn's old, and Gormflaith, whom I suspect of hatching it all out like a pelican's egg, is old—I'll believe it when they send me the cloth dipped in blood."

"If there is one, can I go?" Eoghan said.

"If there's a war, your uncle and I will go, and all the men we can get up, and someone will have to stay here—"

"And take care of Mother," Eoghan said. "And bring in the cows. I know."

Muirtagh looked at him—his head was down on Muirtagh's shoulder. "That's right. Go up to bed."

"Am I to sleep with Finnlaith?"

"Yes."

"Good. He tells me stories."

"Don't you wear him out, you and your stories—you eat stories, the meat's for savory only."

"Good night," Eoghan said.

Aud stood up and made the sign of the Cross over Eoghan and kissed him. "Sleep well," she said.

"Good night, Uncle." He turned and ran out the door.

"Do they never walk?" Cearbhall said.

Muirtagh tossed a chunk of turf into the fire. "How distant you act toward it. When you were, oh, Conall's age, you ran everywhere, but when you tried to walk, you fell flat on your face. Don't you remember? You used to hang on my belt and make me carry you."

"Did I?" Cearbhall said, flushing.

Aud said, "I remember once when Muirtagh wanted to play with you, Cearbhall, instead of being instructed by the elders, and Finnlaith threatened to beat him for it."

"Well, now," Muirtagh said quickly, "that's all gone."

"What's this of a war?" Aud said.

"Oh, it's Maelmordha again. He's sending beyond the—"

"I thought that all settled."

"Settled? Leinster and Munster together?" Cearbhall laughed.

"What is it this time?"

"Oh, this is old. You remember how they were tramping through here last summer, The ó Ruairc and the others."

Aud looked at Cearbhall. "All the summer long he was bringing me strays to feed. He tells me nothing—what is it all about, in the beginning?"

"It's very involved," Cearbhall said. "Not women's business." He looked at Muirtagh. "Were you helping them, then, the rebels?"

"I have friends; when they come panting up to the door, I feed them and let them rest."

"You never told me."

"I just did. They came through the Gap, and some of them knew I was here, so they came—not many, the High King and Maelsechlainn had run them all to tatters. Maelsechlainn knew something of it. You saw the look he handed me in the hall."

"You've not been so shy as I'd thought, up here all this time."

"I keep friends."

"Don't argue," Aud said. "Tell me what started it. Woman that I am, I'm something curious."

Muirtagh shrugged. "When Maelmordha was first the

King of Leinster, he revolted, and he gave the Danes leave to come in and help him, the Danes of Dublin, no others. They fought the High King at Glenmama. Some say it was Maelmordha's bad advice that lost the Danes and Leinstermen that battle. Well, they made it up between them, the High King and Maelmordha, and the High King married Gormflaith, since she was Maelmordha's only sister left unmarried."

"She was married to Maelsechlainn once," Cearbhall said.

"She likes the touch of a King's hands, maybe. Maelmordha went to Kincora—this, some little while ago—to visit the High King. The High King was ready to put Gormflaith aside and may have said so. . . . Anyway, Maelmordha came on the King's son playing chess, and told him to make a certain move. The King's son did. He lost the game for it, too. He and Maelmordha exchanged some very choice insults. Maelmordha walked out of Kincora without a word to the High King and rode straight for Cathair-ni-Ri, and before the High King could do more than shout out the door after him the sword was down off the wall and Maelmordha was storming along the coasts calling up his fighting men."

"It isn't women's business," Aud said. "Women aren't so stupid."

"Maelmordha's a good man, and he's just, but he won't be called a fool by the likes of the King's son."

"Nor would I," Cearbhall said. "He and I are no friends."

"I've heard something about him and I wouldn't care to tell him how to play chess. Gormflaith's been married to two High Kings and a King of Dublin, now, and maybe she thinks she'd like to make another King. She's at the root of it. Sygtrygg's meat for the dog's dish."

Aud shrugged. The baby had fallen asleep long before,

his head against her breast. She lifted him gently, shrugged her shoulder into her bodice, and went off to put the baby in the cradle. Muirtagh shut his eyes, too tired to go after her and climb into bed.

"You named this one Aed," Cearbhall said.

"Yes."

"But you won't—"

"I'm tired. I don't want to talk about it. You're a good man in your own ways, Cearbhall, but you ought to have learned to think about what you're saying. Now, let me go to bed."

"Am I keeping you up?"

Muirtagh smiled. "Good night," he said, and rose.

In the firelight Cearbhall's face looked much younger. "Good night, Muirtagh."

In the morning, with Eoghan and Cearbhall, he rode over to the next glen, where he wanted to move most of the cattle for the rest of the winter. Muirtagh had given Eoghan Cearbhall's old downcountry horse, in a way to make up for forgetting the sword.

On the way over, Cearbhall kept silent, but when they were riding through the valley and Muirtagh had sent Eoghan on ahead to tell the herders they were coming, Cearbhall said, "I don't remember the land we had before the Flight; was it like this?"

Muirtagh shrugged. "Do you remember the land we trapped the King's cousin and the others on?"

Cearbhall thought. "It was like all the land in Meath, no different."

"That was land we held before the Flight."

Cearbhall's mouth fell open. "It was?"

"Did you expect, when you rode over it, the land would open its muddy lips and cry, 'Cearbhall, Cearbhall, here I am'?"

"No, but—"

"How did you imagine I knew that hill was there? We used to play on it."

"Didn't it stir you, to see it again?"

"Yes. I was glad to find a place where we could have some advantage."

"Who has it now?"

"I don't know."

"I thought it bordered on The mac Mahon's land, our old land."

"Oh, God, you know how it goes. One day a clan will say they hold all the land between this point and that, and the next they'll say they'll have nothing to do with those boundaries, theirs are more north."

"Don't you ever want to go back?"

"For years after we came up here nobody talked of anything but going down again, but if I asked them now did they want to, they'd all wail and scream to stay up here."

Cearbhall rode on quietly until they had passed the edge of an ancient slide. He had played there, Cearbhall, when he'd been little; it occurred to Muirtagh that his brother was carefully refusing to admit how familiar were the things of these hills.

At last, Cearbhall said, "I think you're trying to be exactly what . . . just what . . . I mean, that you're trying to do the opposite of what everybody expects of you."

They were coming up on the herders' camp, where the first of the cattle had been brought. Muirtagh swallowed. "I am what I am," he said.

"That's exactly what you are not," Cearbhall said, and rode on ahead, into the midst of the herders.

Muirtagh stopped his pony and stared after Cearbhall, astonished. After a moment the pony moved on, tugging at the bit, and carried him into the camp. Eoghan ran up and pulled at Muirtagh's arm, but Muirtagh only shook him off. "Father," Eoghan said, "what's the matter?"

"Nothing." He slid down.

Liam was up here, and he ran over to Muirtagh. He had ridden the whole of the glen that morning, and he said that the winter rains had soaked the lower end, so that it was boggy.

"It isn't cut or sunken, is it?" Muirtagh said.

"No, but it's very soft."

"I'll go see it later."

He walked out of the camp a way, tasted the grass, and stood looking down the glen toward the low end. In the summer it was dry up here, too dry for good pasture. The hills sloped straight up into the Gap from here; fog like a roof hid the taller peaks.

One of the cows that grazed nearby had a split hoof, and he called out one of the herders and told him to watch it, to see that it didn't lame her permanently. He and the herder, a young boy, walked back into the camp. Cearbhall was talking to the others of the war. He was wearing the face he put on for people he didn't know well, smiling, his big head bowed. "The King of Leinster's called in Sigurd of the Orkneys," he said. "He's a great seafarer."

"And half the Icelanders, probably," Muirtagh said. He got a cup and sipped at the fresh milk in the jug. "How long have these cows been here?"

"Since Christmas, earlier," an older herder said.

"Good milk for cheese."

"He doesn't think there'll be a war," Cearbhall said to the others.

"I never said that. I only said it's no use fighting the Danes until they land, that's all."

Liam said, "But if there is one, we'll go."

"It's known only to God why the batch of you aren't off with the Fenians. Go ask the witch, she'll tell you." To Cearbhall, he said, "She's only a day's ride southwest, and she'll tell you everything you want to know."

The four herders laughed. "More likely," the older man said, "she'll tell you your hands will go warty and your eyes crossed if you don't fetch her food."

"How many of these will calve in the spring?" Muirtagh said, looking over the scattered herd.

"Six," the old man said.

Muirtagh made an effort to remember that and knew he'd forget. "When I ask you again pretend you never told me before. Eoghan, stay here today. Ride down by the boggy part and when you come home tell me if you think we need a brush fence there."

"We—" Liam started, but Muirtagh shook his head at him.

"And be home before dark."

"I told Aoir—" Eoghan said.

"Aoir will be around tomorrow, and whatever you told her you'd show her."

"Well, all right. But make sure somebody takes Blaze up to the loft for Finnlaith."

"I will."

Eoghan went off with Liam. Muirtagh and Cearbhall mounted and rode back toward the home glen.

"Ever since you came back," Muirtagh said, "all the young men are sagging distinctly to the left."

"What?"

"As if they wore swords."

"Well," Cearbhall said. "Eventually everybody has to choose whether he'll be a man or just some cowherd with a field to plow and a litter of pigs by the front door."

"You're showing how little you know of husbandry. We have pens for the pigs, we're wealthy folk."

"You know what I mean."

"But it's so much easier to misunderstand. Do you want to go to the river to check on the fishing, or shall I?"

"Why should—"

"Because somebody has to do it. I can't do everything. Anyhow, you're my Tanist, and if tonight I should un-accountably choke on a fish bone, and with Aud's cook-ing I might, and they laid me out in the cold straw and said prayers over me, brother, I really think you'd find it easier being the chief if you knew where to find the pigs, for example."

"I know where to find the pigs," Cearbhall roared.

"Go down by the river and ride away from the water-fall until you find the men by the nets."

Cearbhall wheeled his horse and galloped off. Muir-tagh laughed after him and rode on down to the stock-ade.

"Muirtagh."

"Unnh."

"Muirtagh, wake up. It's midafternoon and you said you wanted to be woken up." She shook him. He rolled over and burrowed his head into the blankets.

"I'm sleepy."

"You said you wanted to be woken up." She jerked the blankets off him. He snatched at them and she slapped him across his bare feet. "You said you had some-thing to do."

"Tell somebody else to do it."

"Up." She took hold of his arm and wrenched. "Oh, Mother of God. You're like a sack of dirt."

"All right, all right, all right." He swung his feet to the floor and stood up. "Ponies. I'm up. Where's Cearbhall?"

"I haven't seen him since this morning. What did you do with my son?"

"I left him with the herders. He'll be back for dinner." He pulled his tunic over his head and slung his belt around his waist. She went over to look at the baby. He tramped out into the hall, put on his shoes, and walked over to the door.

It looked like rain out, but he thought it always looked like rain at this season. His pony was standing quietly in the shed. That reminded him of the chestnut mare, over in Brefney now, and he realized it was time to send for her. He bridled the pony and led him out.

Most of their ponies were in pasture beyond the river, and every few days they had to be driven down from the trees into the grass. He rode over, looking for Cearbhall on the way, but didn't see him. He found the ponies busily eating the tops off the baby pines, only a little way from their pasture.

"Foolish, idiot animals, why don't you stay where you belong?" The pony stallion, smaller than his black, lunged for him, and Muirtagh whistled, waving his arms. The stallion whirled away and galloped around the far edge of the mares.

The ponies jerked up their heads. Snorting, the stallion trotted importantly back and forth. Muirtagh rode up past him, higher onto the slope, and charged straight down. The whole herd leapt into a mad rush for the low ground. The stallion hurtled this way and that, nipping rumps and running into the laggard mares. Muirtagh slowed, letting them run ahead, and waited.

From the poorer ground above, a neigh blasted, and six or seven bachelors, kept out of the herd by the stallion, raced down after the herd. Muirtagh swung in behind them. The ponies bounced over the rough ground, bounding over rocks and bushes. When Muirtagh trotted out into the pasture, the herd was bunched up near the river, and the stallion was bellowing challenges at the bachelors, drifting a little way off.

Muirtagh rode along the brush fence until he came to the place where they'd knocked it down, grazing across it; with good thick grass right at their feet they always leaned over the fence to eat the few blades growing in the rocks and trees. He dismounted and walked into the trees to find a branch long enough to mend the fence.

When he had found one and dragged it back, Cearbhall was standing there. Muirtagh said, "How's the fishing?"

"Good, they tell me."

Muirtagh laced one end of the branch into the end of the fence, propped the other end up on a rock, and began to thread branches in and out. "I'm tired. Aren't you?"

"Not really."

"Wait until you're my age."

"Are you afraid of The mac Mahon?"

"The mac Mahon? No."

"Who, then?"

"Many many. God, the Devil. Maelsechlainn—"

"Why Maelsechlainn?"

Cearbhall was standing with his hands loose at his sides, his massive shoulders tilted slightly to the left. Muirtagh shrugged. "He's stronger than I am."

"That's no reason to be afraid of someone."

"Oh? It seems logical enough to me."

"Is it Maelsechlainn? Is he why you won't go down and have it out with them, only play harping tricks instead, like some damned—damned servant?"

"Leave me alone, Cearbhall, I'm tired."

Cearbhall put one hand on his shoulder, to whirl him around, and Muirtagh struck at his arm. "Leave me alone!"

Calmly, Cearbhall lifted one fist and hit Muirtagh in the face. Muirtagh flew back and landed on his shoulders, skidding a little; he rolled to his feet and started to charge. Abruptly he caught himself. He straightened up, panting—his jaw hurt and his back. He was shaking as if he had a chill, and it was hard to stand there, not moving.

"Do you always have to be stupid?"

"I'm stronger than you are," Cearbhall said, and lifted his fist again.

"Yes. You're stronger than I am. You go back there and get all the clan together, and tell them you're stronger than I and if they will put me to one side you will be chief and lead them all back down to a glorious revenge, fire in your hands and heart."

He spat out the blood in his mouth. "Go away."

"You know I—"

"I said go away."

Cearbhall lingered, uncertain. Muirtagh bent down after a branch and wove it into the new fence. His mouth filled with blood and again he spat it out. When he looked up, Cearbhall was gone.

He sat down before the fence and put his hands to his face. If he were bigger—if he'd had his bow with him— probably it was God's grace to be little and unable to hurt anybody. He thought about that but the constriction returned to his chest and his throat and he hit the ground with his fist.

Hoofs rattled nearby, and three fillies, never far from each other, galloped past him, squealing and kicking. The stallion was watching them with his ears pricked up. One of the fillies kicked out at another, and they all whirled and fled back to the herd.

Ponies always fought. They picked mates to fight with —the two little bays would graze side by side, until one turned and nipped the other. They'd rear up and thrash at each other with their forelegs until they got tired. Settling down, they'd graze on again, until one nipped the other. . . .

Cearbhall was like a pony. Muirtagh chewed at his knuckle. Revenge. Cearbhall the Pony. I wish he hadn't chosen me to bestow his love taps on.

His black pony was standing hipshot near the fence, reins trailing. The stallion edged nearer, trying to come close to the black without Muirtagh's noticing. Muirtagh got up and walked over.

If she hadn't woken me up like that I'd be in a better mood. Blame everything on Aud; that's what she's there for. He mounted up and rode home.

Cearbhall said nothing about hitting Muirtagh, and Muirtagh's jaw showed only a slight bruise. Aud didn't even ask about it. At dinner, they were civil, and Muirtagh went to bed early.

everal days later, when he woke up in the morning, it was raining. He put his tunic and shoes on and went out into the yard; from the way the rain fell and the direction of the wind he knew it would rain for days. He went back inside.

Aud got up and stirred the fire. "How does it look out?"

"Like the Flood."

"Oh, well. I've got weaving to do."

The men were straggling in for breakfast; they'd tended the horses in the shed. One filled up the box with chunks of turf, and Muirtagh went out again to see how much was left in the storeheap. The three younger children were jumping up and down in the hall when he got back, half in their clothes. Aoir ran over and hugged Muirtagh.

"It's raining," she said. "It's raining—can we hear stories today?"

He picked her up and slung her over one shoulder. She shrieked with laughter. "We'll have all the stories you could possibly want. Whose do you want, mine or your uncle's or Finnlaith's?"

"Yours, Father."

"You've never heard all your uncle's."

Niall and Conall were sitting on the floor; Niall was trying to put on Conall's shoes, but Conall kept kicking them off. The door opened with a great gust of wind and Cearbhall came in.

"The yard's swimming," he said, flinging himself down by the fire. "What must I learn today, Muirtagh?"

"To eat breakfast."

Aud said, "If you'll deign to sit down before the bread goes stale—" She took Conall's wrists in one hand and hoisted him up onto the bench. "Niall, do your laces up all the way."

"Will you tell stories today, Uncle?" Niall said to Cearbhall.

"If you want."

Muirtagh sliced up the bread and meat. "It's going to rain forever." He slapped at Aoir when she snatched for a bit of bread. "Not until we have thanks."

Flann, Liam and Diarmuid, the houseguards, flung in through the door. The rain and wind followed and made a puddle on the floor, and Aud jumped up to slam the door shut. Eoghan dashed in just before the door closed.

"Finnlaith's coming down," he said. "He says he's better now." He forced his way in between Liam and Flann. "Today we tell stories."

"Shall we wait for Finnlaith?" Aud said softly. Everyone else was there.

"I'll go get him. Cearbhall, tell thanks." Muirtagh got up, wrapped his cloak around him, and slipped through the door.

The old man was already coming across the yard, splashing through the puddles. The whole day was grey, and under his cloak Finnlaith was only another grey shape. Muirtagh went over to him and took him by the arm.

"What brings you out?"

"I feel much better," the old man said.

"Let's get inside."

The door flew out of Finnlaith's hands when he opened it, and the rain blew in after them. Muirtagh latched the door. Everyone else was eating. Aoir made room beside her on the bench and screamed for Finnlaith to come sit by her. "Today we'll all have stories," she shrilled.

Finnlaith sat slowly down. He ruffled the little girl's

hair. "It's been long since I saw you, Aoir; what have you been doing?"

Muirtagh signed the Cross over his dish and started to eat. "Fighting," he said. "She fights with them all and when they're beating her screams for Eoghan."

"Oh?" The old man looked at Eoghan. "Defending women already? You'll have enough of that when you marry."

Eoghan laughed. Aud reached over to him and pulled his long yellow hair over his shoulders. "Don't get your hair in your food," she said.

They all finished eating, and Aud made Aoir help her and the other women take the platters off and clean them. The deerhounds came into the middle of the hall and ate the scraps, their long tails wagging. Finnlaith leaned on the table and said, "Now, Cearbhall, we can hear a bit more about how you won such a name for yourself."

"I'm not good at telling stories," Cearbhall said.

"Muirtagh says you spoke right before the Kings, and well."

Cearbhall laughed. "You weren't there to hear Muirtagh play the harp—he had them with their hands in their mouths."

"It was a trick," Muirtagh said.

Conall slid down from the bench and walked unsurely over to the deerhounds. He put his arms around one dog's neck, and the dog licked at Conall's face. Conall sat down abruptly in the midst of the dogs. Muirtagh said, "Maybe we should put a collar on him and take him out to track deer."

"When I was in Munster once," Cearbhall said, "we were fighting against the Danes in Limerick. That was the summer after the winter it rained so much."

"In Limerick or here?" Finnlaigh said. "There was a

winter we had snow to the shed gable. Limerick's always warmer than here."

"Maybe then."

"The second winter after you left here," Muirtagh said. He buttered a thick crust of bread and gave it to Aoir.

"Who was the chief there?" Finnlaith said. "Molloy?"

"The Donovan of Hy Carbery. He and The Molloy were friends a while, all since their fathers killed the King of Munster, Mahon that was the High King's brother. But by the time we came up to fight the Danes at Limerick, they weren't friends any more."

Eoghan put his elbows on the table and rested his chin on his fists, staring at Cearbhall. Muirtagh thought he looked like Aed, his and Cearbhall's father.

"King Brian when he was only King of Munster took Limerick from the Danes. Before he gave it back to them they tried several times to take it back by force, and this time was their strongest try. There was a pack of Danish traders in Limerick, as usual, and they rose up and went with everything they had into the tower and sent for help from Wexford and Waterford."

Aud brought cups and a bowl of usquebaugh and set them in the middle of the table.

"So The Donovan led us all out and we went up to Limerick. It was no problem at all to get inside the gate— every armed man was in the tower—but they shot at us and threw rocks from the high windows, so that we couldn't go in to force open the door."

"Was it on the ground?" Muirtagh said. "The door."

"Yes. This wasn't an Irish monks' tower."

"Oh."

"We sat down outside and waited. At night we built fires and cooked our meat, and by day we sat there and drank and told stories, waiting for them to come out.

"This went on for many days, and it was in the summer and hot and dry. Inside the tower it must have been even worse, because the tower was of stone. After a long while, though, one of the Danes sneaked out to us, through a little hole in the wall around the foot of the tower.

"This was a little man—shorter even than Muirtagh, and not so well set up in the shoulders. He was the base-born son of a high-ranking man from the South Isles or perhaps Man, and he'd failed in everything he'd tried. His name was Thriggi.

"He told us he would lead us in through the hole in the wall, which none of us could find, if we would give him all the goods and ships in the harbor. The Donovan told him he could have everything he wanted, after he'd shown us how to get into the tower, and that night, he did."

"Where was the hole?" Eoghan said.

"It was hidden in the corner of the wall. One big stone had fallen out, but the vines and weeds had grown up about it so high that you couldn't see the stone was out of place. He—Thriggi—said none of the men inside knew of it either.

"So we all sneaked in, in the dead of the night, and got into the tower. I went first up the stair—I had the feeling that would happen which did—and broke down a door at the top of the stair, and we all rushed in on them, sleeping in the middle room of the tower. They jumped up and got their swords and made a circle, but when they saw how many of us there were, they threw down the weapons."

"Danes?" Finnlaith said, surprised.

"These were traders. I only killed one, but The Donovan heard how I had broken down the door and gave me an arm ring for a present—that one in my pack that you've seen, Aud. As for Thriggi—"

He stopped to pour himself usquebaugh. Eoghan pursed his lips, looked all around, and finally banged his fist on the table.

"What of Thriggi, Uncle?"

"Oh, when we'd driven off all the Danes, The Donovan took Thriggi and tied him up and threw him into the harbor, and told him to swallow it all, what he wanted. So you see how traitors are despised on both sides."

They all laughed and leaned back. It made a good story, and Muirtagh sat a moment, enjoying it. Finnlaith said, "That sets me in mind of another story."

So he told that one, which had to do with a man who caught an elf, and the elf tricked the man in much the same way. The man asked the elf to give him eternal life, which the elf did, and went away. But the man hadn't asked for eternal youth, and so he grew older and older, never dying, until he longed to die.

"Now," Finnlaith said, "this man crawls over the world, looking for the cave where, they say, Death sits, and never finding it. So, you see, there's a fitting end to everything, and if a thing should not end, it grows unbearable. So all storytellers should learn."

Without anyone's saying anything, they all stood up and moved over to the fire and sat down around it. One of the women was churning butter, complaining bitterly that it wasn't breaking. Muirtagh got a chunk of wood and a knife out of the keepplace on the right side of the fire, sat down, and started to carve out the body of a doll for Aoir.

"Here's a story with no end to it," he said, "and you needn't bring me my harp. Even these little children know of Iceland, where long ago some Irish fled to escape from the Danes and the Norse, but now the foreigners have conquered it all, too. Now it's said that past

Iceland, the Irish who fled found another country, which they called Great Ireland, and the Danes, so, Irland Mikla. Sometimes I've heard them call it White Man's Land, because there are monks there. I heard all this from the Danes, so it must be true."

He peeled off a long shaving, set the chunk of wood down, and said, "Now, they say that past Great Ireland there's still another country. They've never told me what they call it, but there was a Welsh harper through here not long ago who said it must be the island where Arthur lies waiting. I couldn't find out if any Irish were there, but it always seems that the Danes only go where there are Irish, so maybe there are."

"There are no Irish in Denmark," Cearbhall said.

"There are. They are slaves."

He reached for a cup of usquebaugh. "Brendan the Saint, you know, sailed west thrice fifty days and found the Land of the Young Men, and an Irishman was there before him. I think maybe to the west there is an ocean full of islands, little golden islands under the sun, where all the heroes sleep and where all Irish will find another Irishman's been there before. It's always in the west that they speak of islands, Tir-na-nOg or Irland Mikla. The people off in Normandy and Biscay know nothing of it, I'm told. That's all, there's no story, and no end to it either."

"The end might be that a coward can always find a place to run to," Cearbhall said.

"No. That can't be it. It's been said and well that a coward never finds a place to stop, all the earth's hot coals to the feet of a coward."

He picked up the block of wood again and worked on the legs. Conall staggered over from the heap of sleeping deerhounds and crawled under Aud's skirts, so that only his head showed.

"I sometimes wonder about him," Aud said. She lifted the piece of linen she was working on and peeped over her knees at Conall.

"Tell the Oisin story," Eoghan said.

"You've heard that a thousand times."

"I like it, tell it," Eoghan said.

"There are islands in Oisin's tale, too," Muirtagh said.

"Where did you hear of those islands?" Cearbhall said. "You said from Danes."

"Finnlaith knows. There was that man who crept up to our fires, all wounded, not so long after the Flight—we took him in, not being people to cast anyone out, even a Dane, if he was wounded. He told me some. I heard a bit from a Danish outlaw who was walking from Dublin to Wexford two steps ahead of his reputation—he had everyone's hand against him. And more from the Welsh harper, as I told you."

"I remember him," Finnlaith said. "The wounded Dane—Halfdan was his name."

"Oh, yes," Aud said. "The one who bled so badly over my blankets."

"They were my mother's blankets; that was before you and I married."

"They're my blankets now, and there's bloodstain on them still."

"We keep blankets a long time here," Muirtagh said to Cearbhall. "Niall, fetch me my harp. The Danes taught me Danish, too."

"I didn't know you spoke it."

"Not well. Do you?"

"Oh, some little of it."

Muirtagh played the harp while Finnlaith told the story of Oisin. The rain came down steadily all that day, and all the next, and they all told stories. Muirtagh finished the doll and worked on a bowl he'd told Aud he'd make for her. Now and again he told some tale or another out of the Cuchulain saga.

Finnlaith told most of the stories. Muirtagh had never heard him speak so much. Bending forward, his hands gaunt in the firelight, he called up all the stories he had ever heard in his own childhood—the banshee, elves and fairies, the Aes Sidhe and the Tuatha da Danaan, how Nera found the diadem of the Dagda, how Aengus drew the live frogs from his ears—he made Muirtagh play the Cattle Raid of Cooley, so that he, Finnlaith, could tell that story, too. The children stared at him, their mouths open, seeing what he told them to see. Finally, on the third day, he leaned back and said, "That's all."

"You tell the Sidhe stories best," Niall said. "You must know every story anybody ever heard."

"I'm growing old," Finnlaith said, "or, I should say, I am very old, and old men know far more stories than sprouts like Muirtagh."

"Father isn't a sprout," Niall said.

"Oh, maybe not in age, but he's the smallest man I've ever seen out of our families."

"Dear God," Muirtagh said. "You'd think to listen to you and Cearbhall I stood three fingers shy of the nearest bench."

"You'd been up in the loft too long," Cearbhall said. "Without people to talk to. . . . What's that?"

Muirtagh stood up. "Someone banging on the gate—I thought it was the wind." He took down his bow from the wall. Cearbhall jumped up and they went out together.

"It's probably someone from the low end of the glen," Muirtagh said. Part of the clan had a stockade there.

Flann and Mahon had already gotten to the gate; they called, "There are travelers here, wanting to come in— one's an ollumh."

Cearbhall laughed. Muirtagh waved and shouted, "Let them in." He kept his bow under his cloak, so that the rain didn't wet it.

Three men on drenched horses rode through the gate. Flann and Mahon took the horses off toward the shed, and the three splashed through the mud toward Muirtagh. Cearbhall went to open the door. Muirtagh said, "Welcome in, and you're not strangers. That's Aengus ó Lochain, or I'm nobody."

"Ah," Aengus said. "I'd hoped to catch you out—let you greet me as a stranger and stay hidden for a while."

They shook hands and got inside. Muirtagh glanced up at the sky before he shut the door. "Good, the wrack's flying. It might break up soon."

"Or drizzle on another week or two," Aengus said. "Trying to find you is like hunting a dark horse in a closed shed at night."

The ollumh was unwrapping acres of cloak from his body, showering muddy water over everybody. Aud had a dry tunic out for him, and one for Aengus. The third man, a servant, had gone off with the houseguards, who were drinking and talking at the far end of the room.

"You were looking for me?" Muirtagh said. "Now, we were friends when we were children, and I think I saw you at the Kings' meeting at Cathair, but I shouldn't have thought you'd come hunting me on your own in a flat-out gale. Or is there a Crown behind it?"

"Oh, that, too."

"Don't get talking before the man's warmed up," Aud said. "Both of them. Here, sit down, Aengus."

"Ah," Aengus said, and took the usquebaugh she handed him. "A sensible woman's a boon to any man."

"Aud you know. She's Donnacha's daughter. The various imps and elves on the floor—including the odd-looking deerhound over there—belong to me. And Finn-laith, too, you know—my mother's father. Cearbhall you doubtless know of."

"The Danekiller. You look younger, close on; I'd thought you a wee bit older."

Cearbhall and Aengus shook hands. Cearbhall said, "Sometimes I wish I were."

"Don't; you won't, when you are."

"Cearbhall the Danekiller?" the ollumh said. "I've heard songs about you."

"Don't sing them," Cearbhall said hastily. "It's un-lucky—what harper hates me so much?"

The ollumh smiled—he had a long, thin mouth, and smiling was just pulling back the corners and thinning his mouth even more. "They're good songs, though. My name is Paidrig, I'm of Connaught—I studied with ó Hartigan."

"Oh?" Muirtagh said. "I shouldn't think he'd tutor well, he's so tight wound."

Paidrig nodded. "That's truth."

Aud had given him a cup of warm drink, and he poured himself more. "But to listen to him was a blessing —angels never played so well. Tight wound, yes. He played more with his mind, as if his thoughts had hands. You never heard him."

"No. I've talked to men who have."

"An odd way to judge a man."

Muirtagh shrugged. "Perhaps. And it's most exquisite bad manners to comment on a man's teacher; it equals only making songs about a living man. Ó Flainn I never heard either and I'm no ollumh, but I can play you a fair piece in his style." He turned back to Aengus. "Take care; here goes the fork into the cauldron. Who sent you to me?"

Aengus smiled again. "It was the High King."

"Oh? I thought Maelsechlainn."

"No. The High King wants to know what you meant by that harp play in the hall at Cathair."

"I meant exactly what I said. Why, what does he think I meant?"

Aengus glanced at the others. Muirtagh leaned forward. "They can hear. What I do will make things hard or easy for them, and they should know it."

"He thinks you mean to have them up on hooks, like slabs of meat—some kind of wergeld."

Muirtagh laughed. "No. There's a certain—" he held his hand out flat and tipped it back and forth—"a certain flavor to it, that a man like me should run hot needles into so many great and proper chiefs. But they should recall who put the needles into my hands. What would I do with wergeld? I meant to end it, and I did end it. The feud's over. I like a tidy summing-up. It's the storyteller in me."

He glanced at Finnlaith and said to Aengus, "Sit down."

Aengus moved around the table and sat down. His eyes moved to the ollumh. Muirtagh dragged out the bench a little and sank down on it.

"You know why he sent me," Aengus said. "My clan alone of all of them there was uninvolved—aside from the Ulstermen, of course. And we spent that year together in Mara's house. I'm glad to hear that's what you meant."

"I said what I meant."

"So we all thought, but someone—"

"Maelsechlainn."

"Not he. Someone said that the rancor in it was too deep—"

"Rancor. Oh, God, now, did they think I'd daub them all with honey? They killed my father, they slaughtered my whole clan, all but three or four families. You run back and tell them that I hate them all, but it's over."

"For now," Cearbhall said.

"For good and all." Muirtagh stared at Cearbhall. "There are . . . things in this I doubt my brother understands. I don't think he knows what it's about at all."

Cearbhall jumped up. Finnlaith got him by the belt and dragged him down. The rain rustled in the thatch over their heads, and the wind rattled the door, and for a moment nobody spoke.

"My brother is young," Muirtagh said. "He's not aware yet that there's a difference between the—the trouble a man chooses to get into and the trouble he gets out of the world anyway."

Aengus looked from him to Cearbhall. "Who would be aware of it? There's no choice in it that we can see—the men I'm here for and I. Choice is a King's word, and even they find it hard to say."

"The men you're here for—Kier mac Aodha's one, and Cormac ó Daugherty, and The mac Mahon?"

"The High King sent me. Well, whoever sent me, they—we—expect something of you. Where's the choice?"

"Let them expect. It will give a certain flavor to their hundrum days."

"There is no choice," Cearbhall said. "As Aengus says, it's a thing of honor."

"Aengus never said that. Where there's no choice, what's the honor? You're not only young, you're silly, if you can't see what's breeding in his mind—" Muirtagh stared at Aengus.

"I'll overlook that," Aengus said softly.

"He was your father," Cearbhall said.

"How generous you are," Muirtagh said to Aengus. He swung around, putting his shoulder to Aengus, and stared at his brother. "I'm done arguing with you, explaining to you. I took an oath when I became The ó Cullinane, that while I was chief I would not revenge myself."

"Finnlaith told you to take it. You didn't have to take it—meaching little backbiting oath—"

"He told me what he would do," Finnlaith said. "I said I thought he was right. Who am I to counsel chiefs? Or you, for that matter?"

Muirtagh made his voice soft. "There's a good point. I'm your chief, Cearbhall. You are bound under me—before God, when there are enemies set on every side of him, a wolf or a wild boar would expect to have his kindred and his underlings support him."

His voice had risen to a shout, and he broke off, quieting. Cearbhall with the firelight reaching over his shoulder looked more like Aed than Muirtagh had ever seen—the set of the huge head he remembered especially.

"You've heard it, and heard it, and heard it," he said quietly. "There's no reason for you to hear it again. You may not wish it, but I say you will accept it. There will be no revenge."

Cearbhall's face was shut against him. The words bounced off his head and shoulders. Muirtagh put one hand to his own face. Aed's roaring laughter came echoing through his head. "Half-Aed, you are," he had said to Muirtagh over and again. "Little half-of-me-only." And crushed him in a hug up against his chest, and carried him around in the chair of his crooked arm. "My son." Muirtagh looked at Eoghan, sitting white and still by his mother.

"Do you remember him, Cearbhall? At all?"

"I know he was my father."

"Had he been my father—" Aengus began, and Muirtagh whirled on him and silenced him with a glare.

"You remember him," Cearbhall said. "Is there no outrage in you?"

"Shut up," Eoghan said. His light voice cut in through the others'. He stood up and faced Cearbhall. "Shut up. Shut up. Shut up."

Muirtagh reached across the table and forced Eoghan to sit down. For a moment, half lying on the table, he stared into Eoghan's face. At last he slid back and sat down.

"Shall we go through it again?" he said. He looked at Aengus sitting there with his eyes dancing back and forth between them, and behind him the ollumh with his long hands in his lap. "Yes. And here's company to spread it all over Ireland. What exactly would you have me do, Cearbhall?"

"Why—kill them."

"Oh? Kill all of them? Half the men who were there are dead now, the other half old men. Shall I go among them, one by one, and pull up their long white beards and cut their throats?"

"You twist everything."

"Think on this. How long have we feuded with the mac Mahons? Six generations? Eight? Who remembers why? A cow stolen, a woman refused, a shadow cast over a man's fire, dust kicked over the doorsill. How many have we murdered? As many as they. And you'd start another round of it?"

"You were a Brehon in the womb," Cearbhall cried. He leapt up. "I'll not listen to this. God, you'd have us all on our knees praying for The mac Mahon's long life."

Muirtagh crossed himself. "May God preserve him."

Cearbhall went after his cloak. Aud said, "Where are you going?"

"Away."

Muirtagh said nothing. Cearbhall strode by, flung

open the door, and plunged into the morass of the yard. Muirtagh rose leisurely and went to the door to shut it. He narrowed it to a crack and watched Cearbhall wade across to the horse shed.

"He didn't win his reputation with an easy tongue," Aengus said.

Muirtagh went to the rack where the cloaks were hanging. "Aengus," he said, "an easy tongue could lose you yours, such as it is. Ollumh, you have the freedom of my house while I go set it in order."

"Will you be back soon?" Aud said.

"Yes." Muirtagh went out the door and slammed it.

Cearbhall was just riding out the gate. Muirtagh went into the shed, full of the steaming odor of the rain and the horses, and got his black pony. He trotted through the gate and saw Cearbhall, on the big bay horse, galloping across the glen toward the nearer slope. Muirtagh set the pony into a singlefoot after him.

The horse strode longer than the pony, and at a gallop stretched out a good lead, but in the driving rain and the mud the horse tired quickly. When they'd gone over the hill and were at the edge of the bog, Cearbhall swerved toward the forest, and the pony's steady gait began to cut down the distance between them. When they were almost in the forest, Cearbhall drew up and let Muirtagh catch him.

"What do you want?"

"Your father in you."

Cearbhall wheeled away, and Muirtagh followed. They slid into the forest. The rain fell from leaf to leaf, everything hung dripping in the wind, and the trees hummed like bees. Muirtagh nodded to the north, saying, "There's an old windfall there. We could build a fire."

Cearbhall turned in silence and rode over. They burrowed under the windfall and Muirtagh dug out dry branches and twigs from the deep, rotting shelter of the trunk. Laying out the fire, he lit it with sparks from his dagger.

"When the rain ends, we'll have deer mixed in with the cattle in the pastures," he said. "It's always so after a rain."

Cearbhall chewed on his thumbnail, staring at the miniature fire. Abruptly he turned his head, his eyes on Muirtagh.

"What did you mean back there?"

"Where?"

"When you caught up with me. You said something odd."

"Only that you're like Aed."

"I don't understand you."

"He was big and yellow-headed, like you."

"I mean, I don't understand the way you are."

"Well. Is that so unbearable? I don't understand you either, mostly."

Cearbhall gnawed at the flesh along his thumb. Muirtagh, his arms laid flat over his knees, watched him closely. Finally Cearbhall reached out with the hand he'd been chewing and pushed a long stick into the fire.

"You used to tell me about him, remember? When I was little. I always thought I'd really known him."

"There's something in that. I can remember things that happened before I was born, because Finnlaith told me."

"Was he really like me?"

"Well, he wasn't as solemn as you are, but I suppose that's because he was older. He didn't trust his thinking either." Cearbhall said nothing. "We can't kill all of them, you know. Would you wish to? It's only a dog will lock his teeth in a man's throat and be battered to death."

"They all say it should be done."

"What do you think?"

"I? Think? You said that Aed and I could not think."

"That isn't what I said."

"The same."

"Nobody is going to call you a coward."

"But they'll call you one."

"Oh, certainly, and they'll clear their throats first. Listen to me. You're a known man, and what you say has weight in their councils. But you're young. I don't mean to . . . you're my brother. I want nothing hot or cold between us."

Cearbhall muttered something. He put his head in his hands and kneaded his cheeks with his fingers. "God's love. Do you think I hate you?"

"Of course not."

Cearbhall's hands fell to his lap. "They all say it should be done."

"Yes. And the men who'll say it loudest are the men who murdered Aed and some hundred others of our clan —that's their penance for it. They'd be happier should we try to do it back to them; it would wash the blood from their hands."

Cearbhall frowned, thinking, and finally shook his head. "I don't know."

"I do."

"Aed—"

"Aed would have done it already. But I'm not Aed. Neither are you. So. Let it lie."

"It—is this an excuse?"

"It's the way I feel about it."

"Then you won't fight the Danes."

Muirtagh looked out at the dripping brown wood. "Who's the Brehon now? I'll fight the Danes. I'll kill a man over my own doorstep, if I can."

"What's the difference?"

"Why go hunting for someone to kill? That's all. I'll sit quietly at home and play my harp, and when the Danes come I'll put enough arrows in them that their own wives couldn't tell them from a cloth to stick pins in. I'm mild as a deer, my tongue's made of honey, but I'll defend what's mine."

"I don't see the difference."

"I do, and I want you to obey me."

"I'm all confused." He shook his head. "My mind's all jumbled up."

"It's a common thing with young men. Especially young men who are heroes." Muirtagh tapped his fingers on his knee. "I still wonder why Aengus came."

"Why? He said the High King sent him."

"The High King's a man of the Dal Cais. Aengus is from Meath. Brian hardly knows him, not to send him on an errand of this sort—to make up the High King's mind for him, when his own's made up by chance remark on the highway and changed with the next thing he hears?"

"Then who else?"

"Kier, Cormac, Dermot mac Mahon—the reason's the same. Come on, let's go back. I'm cold."

When they rode into the yard, the rain stopped. Flann came out of the house to take the horses. Through the open door they could hear the ollumh's deep voice, singing; Muirtagh cocked his head to listen.

"He has something of ó Hartigan in him," he said.

"As long as he sings nothing of me."

"He won't. Come along inside."

They walked into the house. Aud looked up and smiled, and Finnlaith leaned back with a sigh. Aengus only looked thoughtful. The ollumh closed his song.

"We'll have Dierdre's tale," Muirtagh said, "if you know it all. There are parts in it I can't remember well. Eoghan, fetch me my harp."

* * *

At dawn the next morning, Aengus and his ollumh and his servant rode out. Muirtagh took an axe and a wedge and went off behind the shed to cut wood. It was just after dawn and the low clouds were streaming off across the sky; in the blue air the sounds of birds were harsh and clear, each one ringing separately. Muirtagh laid out the logs and began to split them.

Cearbhall came out, after the sun was well up, and led out his new horse. He hitched it to the shed and went back inside for a brush and currycomb.

"It's cold," he said, coming out. He went to work on the horse's coat.

Muirtagh straightened up; his back ached. "Not so cold as it could be. It's the wet that gives it the edge." He took the axe by the throat, kicked a chunk of wood around until it lay flat, and went around and began to swing. A chip flew up and hit the horse.

"Whoa," Cearbhall said. "Whoa, now. Whoa, there. Do we need meat? I thought to go out hunting."

"The herders will bring in a deer or two. No reason. If our grass hurts the soles of your feet so much, there's an errand you could do for me, all off in Connaught."

Niall and Conall ran out of the house toward them, whooping. Muirtagh stood up to watch. Conall fell down, picked himself up out of the mud, and ran on after Niall; Niall stopped by Muirtagh.

"Mother says—"

"While you're here, you might gather up the chips." Muirtagh bent down and swiped at the mud on Conall's shirt front. "What does she say?"

"You should go and see Finnlaith, he's sick again." Niall began to pick up the chips of wood, making a pouch out of his tunic.

Cearbhall said, "He's old—how many men see their

great-grandsons?''

Muirtagh pulled Conall away from the horse's heels. ''Will you go to Connaught for me?''

''Yes. Where?''

''Wait until I've seen Finnlaith.''

Muirtagh went over to the house and climbed up into the loft. Finnlaith was in his bed, with Aud sitting beside him. She looked up.

''It was the rain,'' she said. ''He's fevered.''

Muirtagh put his hand on the old man's forehead, hot and dry as parched earth. Finnlaith stirred slightly and Muirtagh drew away a little.

''I'll send for a monk.''

''Do you think—''

''Like enough. Will you stay here with him?''

''Yes.''

''Or Eoghan. Someone.''

She turned her face away from him. ''Yes.''

He lingered a moment, trying to hope that Finnlaith might get better, and finally went down to the yard again. Cearbhall had saddled up his horse and was riding around the yard, slowly, with Conall on the withers in front of him and Niall hanging on behind. Conall screamed at the top of his lungs and the horse shied.

''How is he?'' Cearbhall said.

Muirtagh stood by the horse's shoulder, absently pulling his mane. ''Maybe he'll get better. It's God's will.''

Conall reached down for Muirtagh, and Muirtagh lifted him off the horse, holding him in the crook of his arm. Niall said, ''Is Finnlaith dead?''

''No.''

''He's an old man,'' Cearbhall said.

''You keep telling me that. You'll be old, too. I'm something used to him, and poor weak-headed man that I am I like his advice on things. The ó Ruairc will be in

Brefni, some little way past the Upper Lough. Ask any-one there. The cairns mark the path through the Gap. If it gets foggy, stop still and wait until—anyway. Tell The ó Ruairc about Aengus and that the High King is bring-ing me into it. Especially what Aengus said. Have him tell Maelmordha."

"Maelmordha? We'll be fighting him."

"So we will. Maelmordha is a clever sort who can hold more than one idea in his head at once."

Niall slid off the horse and leaned on Muirtagh, watch-ing him pull the horse's mane. Muirtagh said, "My chest-nut mare is at Brefni. Bring her back. That's mostly why you're going."

"Isn't that far?" Niall said. "To send a mare to be bred."

Cearbhall dismounted and went into the house after his gear. Muirtagh ruffled Niall's hair. "Our horse stock is runty and The ó Ruairc's, God bless them, could be taken for small hills if they'd only stand still long enough."

"Is The ó Ruairc our friend?"

"That depends on whom you're talking to. I wouldn't want you running up to the High King and shouting that The ó Ruairc is my friend."

"Why?"

"Something you'll find out when you grow up."

Cearbhall came out with a pack, lashed it across the horse's withers, and mounted. Muirtagh stood back.

"Watch that road through the Gap, and be careful all the way. The King's peace is the King's peace, but I shouldn't like to see the King's war, for all that."

Cearbhall grinned. "I'll stay out of the bog, I'll watch out for thieves, I'll cross myself at sundown and stay away from women in armor." He started off, waved at the gate, and banged it shut behind him.

"Niall, go get Liam. He should be over near the pony herd. Tell him to ride to Kevin's Church and ask them if they will send a monk up here."

Finnlaith did not wake up. Aud could feed him only a little at a time, holding his head on her knee while she spooned broth between his lips. Sometimes he lay still, sometimes he thrashed about, crying and pounding the bed with his fists, but always he fevered. His skin began to flake off, and his hair was dull and dry. Aud prayed, and made Aoir and the boys pray. The baby she left with a woman in one of the other houses.

The monk came in that afternoon, a husky man burned black by the sun; Liam said he had walked fast enough to keep up with the pony even at a jog.

"God's grace on you," the monk said to Muirtagh. "The abbot asked me to thank you for the sheep you sent us."

"He thanked me when I went down for Christmas."

The monk smiled. "Are you suspicious of thanks? They're grateful, and so am I, for their sakes."

"You aren't from the monastery school?"

"I wander. Clonmacnois is my home, if I have one."

He climbed up the ladder, his wide feet confident on the rungs, and sniffed at the air. The three boys were beside the bed, and Muirtagh sent them away. Aud drew back into a corner.

"God be with us here," the monk said. He sat down and put one huge hand on Finnlaith's cheek. "How long has he been like this?"

"Since two mornings ago," Aud said. "During the rain he was hale. But before he was sick."

Finnlaith looked shockingly older than he had the day before. The monk sat a moment, looking at him, and Muirtagh could tell by the line of the big man's shoulders what he thought.

"Is this your father?"

"My grandfather."

"Has he wakened at all?"

"No," Aud said. "He raves, now and then."

"Fetch me some water."

She brought him the pail from the corner, and the monk scooped up a handful of it, made the Cross over the water, and, murmuring, anointed Finnlaith's forehead, lips and breast. Down at the foot of the ladder, one of the dogs whined to be carried up.

"Shall I send the children up?" Aud said.

The monk smiled, said nothing, crossed himself, and with his eyes on Finnlaith's face sat still, only his lips moving.

The air in the loft seemed intolerably hot and damp. Muirtagh went to one corner of the loft and made a hole in the thatch, trying to keep Aud from seeing him do it. But she saw.

He went down into the yard. He finished cutting the wood. Conall and Aoir came over to watch him and asked him to settle a dispute between them.

"It's Aoir's doll," Muirtagh said to Conall.

"It isn't that, Father. Look. He took the leg off."

She produced the leg and the doll's body, tried to fit the leg back on, and with a shrug held up the two parts in her hands toward Muirtagh. He took the doll and sat down on a log. The doll's legs and arms were bound to the body with straws, and the straw had broken; the end had slipped back inside the hollow body where all the straws were knotted together. He fished it out again with a splinter and tied on the leg.

"There."

Aoir took back the doll and patted it doubtfully. She gave the leg a tug. "Tell Conall not to take it."

"I've already told him."

Muirtagh looked hard at Conall, and Conall frowned
thunderously. Aoir went off, talking to her doll. Muirtagh picked up Conall and carried him on his shoulder
into the house.

Aud was sitting beside the fire, her hands in her lap,
staring. All the others, children, men and women, were
gone, and in the growing dusk inside the house Aud
looked old and her back seemed bent more than even an
old woman's.

"You think he's going to die," she said. "I saw you
make the hole in the thatch."

"What does the monk say?"

"He's laid him on the floor."

Muirtagh shrugged. Conall had gone out again, and
Muirtagh sat down by the fire and put his feet up to it.
"Will you bring me something to drink?"

She rose silently and brought him a noggin of usquebaugh and hot water. When she had sunk down again
beside the hearth he said, "You take this too close to the
heart. He wouldn't want this from you."

"Oh, well." She brushed back a long wisp of hair. "It's
only that I'm so tired."

"Tired? Why?"

"Now, you ask me that? You and Cearbhall going at
each other, and Eoghan wild about the whole thing, and
that silken Aengus—ah." Her hand moved impatiently.
"That's all."

He drank the usquebaugh. "If you're tired, sleep."

"I've told you why I'm tired and sleep won't help.
Stop fighting with Cearbhall."

A woman came in the door, carrying the baby. "I
thought you'd want him back before dark, Aud. He's
just the quietest, sweetest baby I've ever seen."

Muirtagh smiled fleetingly. Aud took the baby and
joggled him a little. The women bent over him and

crooned and made slurping noises at him. They reminded Muirtagh of Aed with babies. Aed had loved children, all children.

Finnlaith, now, when he was a younger man had ignored the children—Muirtagh remembered that. He and his sister when she was alive and Aud, who had then been only another of the children, and the rest of them, had played uproariously in the yard with Aed, but Finnlaith would brush them off when they tried to talk to him, chase them away, even slap at them. Aed and Finnlaith had been about the same size, but in Muirtagh's memory Aed's face was always on a level with his own, and young Finnlaith's so far above that he'd had to throw his head back all the way to see.

"The children will miss him," Aud said, now that the woman was gone.

"I can't remember when he wasn't living in our house, here or down on the plain."

"Do you remember how he played with us when we were children?"

"Played with us? No, that was Aed. Finnlaith never did."

"Surely it was Finnlaith."

But she wasn't certain. He watched her a moment, studying her face, making himself recognize her, see her face as if he'd never seen it before. "You know," he said, "I could have gotten a lot worse for a wife."

"Oh." She made the impatient gesture again, but she was smiling. "Do you remember how you used to pull my hair and make me think it was Máire?"

"Um-hum."

A few of the women came in and began to get the dinner ready. Muirtagh and Aud only sat still and looked at each other and smiled, with the women bustling and chattering around them. At last he rose and went outside, to go up to the loft and see how Finnlaith was.

The next day he and most of the other men moved the cattle into the winter pasture, driving them slowly over the hill and across the arid upland end of the next glen. Eoghan he sent to check on the sheep at the far end of the home glen. When they all came back in the midafternoon—half the men going off toward the other stockade —Eoghan came out the gate to meet them. Muirtagh could tell by his face that Finnlaith had died.

He dismounted and gave Liam his pony to put up, and Eoghan came over to him.

"Finnlaith is dead," the boy said.

"Yes. I know."

"The monk wants to talk to you."

"Where is he?"

"In the house."

The monk was sitting at the table with Aoir on his lap, braiding her doll's hair. When he saw Muirtagh he put the little girl down on the bench beside him, patted her head, and got up, and he and Muirtagh went into a corner.

"You have my sympathy," the monk said.

"Thank you." For what? he had almost said. He couldn't hold it in his mind that Finnlaith was dead; the words bewildered him, and the thought slipped out of his grasp and swam back in. The monk's dark eyes showed that he guessed at it.

"He was very clear for a while, just before he died. He asked for you, and I told him you were out. He said that was good." The monk smiled faintly. "Now, he said that you should keep Cearbhall away from The mac Mahon, and that you should keep the oath, whatever that means."

"For that we hide in corners? Excuse me."

"No. He was worried about something, and I mislike leaving a man to die worrying, so I said I would ask you if there was anything I could do for you. He seemed to think you needed support against your brother."

A flicker of anger touched Muirtagh, and he felt guilty at it. "No. I don't think so. We've settled that, my brother and I."

"I only mentioned it because he asked me to."

"Yes."

"It—"

The monk broke off and looked at the wall, frowning. His short nose wrinkled.

"Sometimes I think dying men catch glimpses of things. He was worried and I don't think it was about a simple family quarrel."

"This isn't simple."

"I know the story of it." The monk's eyes turned toward him. "Should you ever have need of an ear to run your words through, mine are as good as a blind wall's."

Muirtagh shrugged. "I think it's all settled now."

"Good."

He went back to Aoir and the doll. Muirtagh stared after him. Eventually, Aud came over and made him go sit on a bench, and when she did, she gave him a little shake. The shake and what the monk had said made him realize that Finnlaith was dead in a way that Eoghan's words hadn't.

They ate dinner, and Aud spread out a blanket on the floor, next to the fire. Four of the men and Muirtagh and Eoghan went up to the loft and carried Finnlaith's body down and laid it out on the blanket. People from the other stockade came into the house; Aud had sent two men down to tell them Finnlaith was dead almost before the monk had come down the ladder to tell her. Two by two, the women washed and combed Finnlaith's hair and put on his best shirt.

Muirtagh sat beside Eoghan next to the fire, wishing that Cearbhall had come home. When Finnlaith had been laid out properly everyone began to drink and talk, standing in clumps. The loft could not be slept in for three days, and Aud put the younger children to bed in her and Muirtagh's room; Eoghan and the monk were to sleep in the other. Muirtagh made Eoghan drink a great cup of usquebaugh, and the boy grew tired at once and went tamely off to bed.

As soon as he decently could, Muirtagh left the house and went outside, walking as far as the shed. It was foolish to believe that Finnlaith had been foresighted because the monk did, when the monk could have gotten it wrong. Dying men sometimes took great pains over small things, and Finnlaith had been feverish.

Standing by the shed he felt suddenly crowded, as if an invisible progress were swarming past and around him. He stiffened and the feeling increased. The air was thick and almost jostled him. They might be tapping him on the shoulder, elbowing him in the ribs, poking him. His stomach contracted. He shut his eyes for fear he might see something and took a step toward the house. He took another step. The feeling packed his mind, forcing out all his denials. Something laughed at him. He opened his eyes suddenly and saw nothing but the oddly luminous dark. When he looked at the sky he saw the moon like a single malevolent eye staring at him.

He took three more steps toward the house, looked into the northern sky, and there saw the faint strokes of armor-light dancing, just beyond the hill. They faded, flashed brilliantly, and faded again. He plunged for the house and barely kept himself from slamming the door.

Everyone was in bed. The guests from the other

stockade were lying on the floor around the fire. For a blind moment he thought he had been out in the dark half the night, that the swarms and the lights had held him still for half the night. But Aud came out and beckoned to him, and she hadn't taken off her clothes. He imagined them all, talking and drinking, cheerful, warm, while just outside his own house the un-Christian hostings held him captive, but it wasn't so, Aud would have come for him.

"Everybody's asleep," she said softly, and shut the door behind him.

He sat down on the bed, unlaced his leggings and shoes, and put them down softly so the three children in the bed wouldn't wake up. Aud hung her clothes on a peg; she climbed into the bed with a rustling of the straw. He could hear her murmuring her prayers.

When he lifted his arms to take off his tunic his muscles ached. He tossed the tunic down and crawled in beside Aud.

"Good night," he whispered, and began his prayers.

"Mother."

"Go to sleep, Aoir," Muirtagh said. With five in the bed it was close.

"Niall's kicking me."

Muirtagh burrowed his head into the mattress. Aud said, "Go to sleep, he'll stop."

The straw crunched and sighed. Aoir had climbed over Aud and was squeezing in between her and Muirtagh. It's nothing less than an act of God that we ever had more than one, he thought. It occurred to him that he was the oldest man in his family. He shut his eyes. The breathing around him was a chorus. The whole room was full of the sound of breathing. When he was sure Aud was asleep, he got up, took his cloak off the peg, and went out into the big room to sleep on the floor.

They moved Finnlaith in his shroud down to the burying ground the next morning. The shroud was of linen; Aud had woven it. Laid out on the stilts, Finnlaith waited under the sky while Muirtagh dug his grave, while the people passed by to look and pray. The sky was blue and the air was cold.

Eoghan came out and sat by watching Muirtagh dig the grave. The ground was hard frozen only a little below the grass. Muirtagh took an axe to it, wary of stones, to hew out the grave. Eoghan sat cross-legged a little way away and stared at nothing. Muirtagh straightened up, wheeled his arms, and looked down at the hole he'd made. It was deep enough for a winter grave.

"Father?"

"Ummmm." He got down into the grave and shaped it with the spade.

"I'll die. Won't I?"

"We all die, Eoghan."

The boy said nothing. Muirtagh finished the grave and jumped out. Two of the old women were praying beside Finnlaith's body. Muirtagh gathered up his tools, took them in one hand, and bent down to draw Eoghan to his feet. Eoghan stood all in a rush, his arms around Muirtagh, and pressed his face to Muirtagh's shoulder. Muirtagh ruffled his hair. Putting his arm along Eoghan's back, he started off, the boy half walking and half dragging along with him. They passed the women praying, and the women began to keen.

Cearbhall came back in the early morning, in mist like woodsmoke, bringing another man on a big Kerry stallion with him. Muirtagh went out when he heard the sentry's call and waited beside the door. The two riders.

with the chestnut mare on a leadline, walked their horses into the yard. Cearbhall's hood was down on his back but the stranger was hooded like a witch. Muirtagh went over to them.

"I brought you a guest," Cearbhall said. "The ó Ruairc has some messages for you. How's Finnlaith?"

"We buried him three days ago." Muirtagh looked up at the hooded man. He could see only the man's nose and the faint glitter of his eyes, but seeing his long hands, he knew him. "Do you sit so silent, Maelmordha? Here's the second odd visitor I've had since Cathair."

Maelmordha laughed. Throwing back his hood, he said, "Your eyes don't belong in a man's head. I was at The ó Ruairc's, and when your brother came, I thought of leaving with him."

"Are you going to Leinster?"

"What of Leinster's left to me."

"Well, you shouldn't stop, man, especially not with me. Cearbhall, put up the horses, it's cold."

Muirtagh held Maelmordha's reins. Cearbhall dismounted and led off the horses. Muirtagh, his eyes on the chestnut mare, lingered by the door.

"Are you so unsafe?" Maelmordha said.

"Pfft. The Kings' people buzz around me like bees in a dead cow's eyes. You'd think I led a thousand men, and all of them my brother for the long arm."

"I heard you had them by the roots of their eyes at Cathair."

"So; but it wasn't my doing. It was theirs." He looked at Maelmordha's horse, which Cearbhall was haltering. "You ride high now. The ó Ruairc must be biting on his beard."

"He offered me ten cows, five stallions, and two mares in foal—one of them was yours, I think. When I said no he went cross-eyed and the smoke dribbled out of his ears. He's a good horse, but devilish hard on my hosts' tempers."

"Oh, I have a black pony I might trade for him, do you add a tuath to graze him on. The ó Ruairc's dam was a red mare, they say, and that's why he'd rather have a good horse than go to Heaven when he dies."

Maelmordha looked off. "At the moment I'd take your black pony in trade for my sister, frankly."

"Gormflaith."

"Oh, which of my sisters makes trouble but Gorm-flaith?"

"Aud wouldn't let me. Take her in trade, I mean. Come inside."

They went in. Aud and the children were up, and Con-all was crawling toward the deerhounds. Muirtagh almost tripped over him, not noticing him. "Aud, come get this brat."

Aud came over, scooped up Conall, whistled to the hounds, and brought them all to the fire. Aoir and Niall were sitting on the bench, staring at Maelmordha, and Aud kept shooting him oblique glances.

"Eoghan," Muirtagh said, "take your brothers and sister outside and play in the yard. Or do your chores. Better the chores."

Cearbhall came in, past a flood of children, and sat down. "It's a hard ride."

"Especially at night," Muirtagh said. Aud came over, a platter of meat for breakfast in her hands.

"Do you wish me gone?" she said softly.

"Well, you have the baby to feed."

She muttered something. The platter almost fell to the table. Aud stalked off across the room; the sleeping-room door slammed after her. Maelmordha and Cearbhall speared meat from the platter and cut bread. Muirtagh stood up.

"I'll put some shoes on; you hauled me out of my bed, night riders that you are. Cearbhall, fetch some wine for the—for him. And tell Eoghan that they may all eat at Brendan's house."

He went back into the sleeping room; the door was not quite latched. Sitting down on the bed, he drew on his shoes and laced them. Aud with the baby at her breast ignored him. When he was going out the door he turned and said, "Do your ears sprain, tell me, I'll rub liniment on them."

She glared. He shut the door, tripped the latch, and went back to the table.

"Did you say your grandfather had died?" Maelmordha said.

Muirtagh nodded. "It was the wet, I think. He hadn't been so well that I could have hope for him past this winter anyway."

"I'm sorry for it. I'd wanted to talk to him."

"Is that what you're after? Deep speech?"

Cearbhall, sipping wine, looked sharply at them.

"Oh, well," Maelmordha said. He leaned back, drawing his long brown hands over the table top. "I heard something of what you did at Cathair-by-Tara. I'd have you with me, if you'd come."

"Not with the Danes," Cearbhall said.

Maelmordha ignored him. Staring at Muirtagh, he said, "You have all the arguments for it already."

"Muirtagh—"

"Cearbhall, be quiet." He looked back at Maelmordha. "I cannot. You know all the arguments for that, too."

"I didn't know when they spoke to me, Sygtrygg and Gormflaith, that they meant to bring in the Orkney Jarl. I swear I did not."

"Maelmordha, you always mean as well as any man.

You're just not lucky, that's all."

Maelmordha's flexible mouth twisted into a smile, and his eyes moved toward Cearbhall and back again to Muirtagh. "You must admit," he said mildly, "that I give Irish advice to the Danes, at least."

Muirtagh laughed. "And you play a bad game of chess. Those two things every man in Ireland knows about you."

"What do you owe them that you won't come with me? Faith?"

"I owe them nothing. Don't think I'm so mild I've not thought of having their hides off for it."

"I know. We spoke of it once, remember? Then I thought you wise and moderate, but now . . . So does a man think with his sword hand." Maelmordha smiled. "I was surprised that they held the council at Tara. Maelsechlainn's to his chin in it, obviously."

"Ah, no. Don't misjudge it. It's nothing of Maelsechlainn's. He's there because of the foreigners that will come to help you, and if it weren't for the Orkney Jarl and the rest, he'd be somewhere else. He'd no more help the High King than me, and it's gall to him that he is."

"I had a different impression."

"Well, that's how I see it, and I have no sword hand to think with."

"That's so. That's so." Maelmordha's mouth twitched. "Or is a string hand as wise?"

"Wiser. Only two fingers draw the string, and the rest are left entirely to think."

Maelmordha laughed.

"If Maelsechlainn were much part of this, even though you brought all Denmark and Norway down on us, I would not move to help him. I'd do what I did in the last war, you know, tend my herds and—"

"Take us in," Maelmordha said roughly. "Feed us and throw your own children out of their beds so we could sleep."

Cearbhall's head jerked.

"But this is the High King's and he took the trouble to hunt me out, call me to his council." Muirtagh ran his hands over the table. "You see how it is."

"Yes." Maelmordha's long dark face was solemn. "You still don't see, do you? They won't let you alone. Maelsechlainn might. But the little ones, The mac Mahon and the others, they won't have it from you, what you're trying to do. Lord Jesus, you've made them criminals."

"They'll have it or choke to death on it. Either way."

Cearbhall cut a bit of meat and put it in his mouth. Muirtagh glanced at him.

"What can they do against me? Massacre us again? No, they'd need a King for it, as they did the last time. Maelsechlainn will let it go. I don't bother Maelsechlainn."

"You do."

"I do not."

"I don't know. I don't know."

"If you think on it you'll see I'm right."

Maelmordha looked down at his wine, across at Cearbhall, and stared at Cearbhall a long while.

"He's keeping quiet," Muirtagh said. "We had it all out a while ago."

"He told me."

Muirtagh glanced at Cearbhall, who refused to look anywhere but at his winecup. "Oho," Muirtagh said. "I see it now."

Maelmordha said nothing, only smiled.

"Well, I'll give you my best sleeping room all to yourself, and we can talk all night, but for both our sakes I think you should sleep and ride on."

"You're so jittery."

"I can't keep my household out of doors forever. Do they know you're in the habit of jogging over the countryside? The Kings, I mean. If they don't, better they should not."

"Yes," Maelmordha said. He stood up. "I'm tired."

Muirtagh led him off. "I'll admit it's as much for my sake as yours, but you're odd to be roaming."

"I have to know things."

"And you can't send men about?"

"It's to the King of Leinster to do the King of Leinster's work."

Muirtagh studied him and smiled. "I know. Should the day come when you're running and Leinster's shut to you, come here."

They went into the empty sleeping room, and Muirtagh shut the door. The light was dim in the room and he could hardly see Maelmordha's face.

"For your sake I wouldn't come here if everything but hell and here were shut," Maelmordha said. "I'd as soon you were no victim of mine. But when the time comes that you're running, Muirtagh, come to me."

Muirtagh smiled. "You're more set in your thinking than you used to be. Sleep well. If you need anything, call me."

He went out. Cearbhall waited for him to come to the front doorway, and, when he did, hissed, "Why do you even listen to him?"

"We were friends before you were ever born. If I want to listen to him when he's wild with the idea he'll be beaten, that's for me to decide."

"You think he—"

"Oh, I imagine he'd rather be beaten by us than by the Danes. If he and the Danes beat the Kings, the Danes will turn on him, and he knows it."

"Then why did he ally with them?"

"You heard him. Sygtrygg's his nephew, and Syg-trygg's King of Dublin, if not an Irish King at least a King in Ireland. He said he never knew they'd call in the Orkney Jarl and the others."

"What others do you think they'll bring?"

Muirtagh stood in the fresh sunlight. The mist was vanishing. "All the swords and axes in the Southern Isles. Every ship that coasts Ireland and England, every Ice-lander who's tired of being a farmer, every—"

"You make it sound like the whole world."

"The Orkney Jarl has a great name."

Eoghan was standing in front of them, waiting for Muirtagh to finish. "Father, can we shoot arrows today?"

"Is the barn clean?"

"Yes, Father."

"And the horses brushed, and all the trash out of the gutters on the house, and you've carted off the leaves up against the wall, over behind the barn."

"Well . . . all but the leaves."

"Good. We'll do some shooting."

"I'll go look at Finnlaith's grave, I think," Cearbhall said.

"When you're done, there are some leaves piled up—"

"I'll attend to it." Cearbhall laughed and strode off.

"Who's that other man, Father?"

"I could tell you he's a horse-trader come in from Connaught with your uncle." Muirtagh led him into the house to fetch their bows.

"That isn't so," Eoghan said.

"Now, how do you know?"

They went through the gate and started around to-ward the back of the stockade, up toward the waterfall.

Eoghan said, "I remember him. He was here last summer."

"I think it's better you don't know who he is."

"Oh, Father."

In the field under the cliff, there was little grass, little sunlight. Muirtagh had made a target on a beech tree there with his dagger, back when they'd first come to this glen, and the target had become pitted and scarred, so that it stood out clearly on the tree trunk. Some time later he'd hung an old wooden shield rimmed and bound in iron from a low branch, and now he swung it back and forth, to see if the cord was still sound.

Eoghan soon tired of shooting at the tree and they shot at the shield, which swung when an arrow struck it, whirling, so that they had to wait for the broad surface to start turning toward them and shoot quickly before it turned away. Eoghan could pack arrows into the tree but he had never hit the shield.

"You do it, Father. Let me watch."

Muirtagh strung his bow. "It's a trick, and there's nothing useful in hitting shields." He drew out an arrow. "Remind me to make more arrows before the winter's out. Do we have any owl feathers left?"

"Some."

"There's nothing I'm fonder of than hunting owls in the dead of winter." He raised the bow and shot. The shield spun madly.

"Oh," Eoghan said. "You hit it." He sounded disappointed.

"You have to judge how long it takes the arrow to get there, that's all. It's a pretty trick, shooting at something that isn't here yet."

"That's what you do with a deer."

"Not this way, quite." He shot again; the shield

rocked and whirled. "And you'll waste arrows if you try to kill running deer. It's easier to get close while they're standing still or grazing."

He shot again, and the shield bounced back and forth. Eoghan threw down his bow. "I'll never do it."

"Pick up your bow. You will."

"I won't."

Muirtagh cuffed him lightly on the shoulder. "Are you Aoir or Eoghan?" He went off after his arrows. Eoghan trailed him, the bow dragging along behind him.

When they were close enough to see the shield plainly, Muirtagh stopped and hissed his breath out between his teeth. "Now, you see? Being too clever has its own punishments." One of the arrows had struck another and ruined it. "In all that shield it could have found another place to go." He pulled out the arrows, cut the head off the ruined one, and tried to salvage the feathers.

"Does Uncle shoot a bow, Father?"

"Uncle's a downcountry man."

"No he isn't."

"He's a swordsman."

"Which is better?"

"Well, a bow's nothing to carry into a close fight, but a man with a sword can wave it all he will from fifty paces and never hit a thing."

He cased up the arrows. "A sword is for fighting with. Remember Halfdan—the Dane who came by and told us stories? He could have told you more names for a sword than there are in your head for any one thing. The Danes almost marry their swords."

The boy sat down on his heels and picked up one of his arrows. The head was scored along the edge. "See? I hit it, at least."

"You're a good shot. You'll do well enough."

They went back and Eoghan shot more arrows. Muirtagh spread his cloak on the ground and sat on it. Eoghan shot grimly, but he'd already learned not to be angry at his bow. That had been Aed's mistake; when he'd done something wrong, he'd brooded over it, boiling.

Eoghan let out a whoop that almost lifted Muirtagh off the ground. "I hit it, Father—look. See? I hit it."

"Let's go see."

They ran down to the tree. The shield was still swaying when they reached it, and one of Eoghan's arrows, the red-dyed one, thrust out of the edge near the iron.

"It's not in the center," Eoghan wailed.

"Pfft. It's there, that's what matters. Later you can cry if it's not in the center."

"I'm going to shoot until it hits the center."

"No you aren't. We're going back. You'll shoot better tomorrow than you will after this."

"Oh, all right."

They went back to get Muirtagh's cloak and arrow case. Eoghan said, "Father, what was the Flight like?"

"The Flight?"

"You've never told me. I know they killed us all. But what was it like?"

"Nothing that's interesting to hear about."

"Oh, Father, tell me. How old were you?"

"Your age, about."

"Was Mother in it?"

"Yes."

"Oh, Father, please?"

" 'Oh, Father.' Ask your mother."

"She won't tell me either."

"Good. I always knew I married her for some reason. Ask your uncle."

"But Uncle was only a baby."

"He'll tell you if you ask him. Oh, stop it, Eoghan. Here you are, standing as high as my shoulder, and you act like Conall when he wants something. I—"

He stopped. They were almost to the stockade gate, and through it he saw horsemen in a herd before his front door, and he recognized them at once. "Eoghan, go get a pony out of pasture and ride for the herders."

Eoghan looked into the stockade, turned, and ran.

Muirtagh took a deep breath and went through the gate. The mac Mahon was leaning down from his horse, talking to Aud. She stood in the doorway, her hands pressed to her skirt, and when The mac Mahon had stopped speaking in his ugly, smirking voice, she said, "They aren't here. If you would fight with women and some small children, we could accommodate you there."

Her voice was steady. Muirtagh strung his bow and nocked an arrow. His hands were clammy. He stepped through the gate and put his back to the fence.

"The man is here," he said. "Do you wish any more, Dermot, we could call them up, but I think you'll find me alone enough for the pack of you. Is the winter so fat to the north that you can come down and raise the dust in my dooryard?"

The horsemen twisted around, ashamed that they hadn't seen him come in. Dermot mac Mahon crowded his horse forward. "So there you are, serpent tongue."

Muirtagh's knees were wobbling. "Here I am, sheep's brain. No, don't come any nearer. I like you where I can see you. Oho, it's the King's cousin, too, come all this way to court my woman."

Kier mac Aodha flushed. Muirtagh glanced all around the compound, looking for Cearbhall, and, not seeing him, turned to Dermot again.

"Now, kindly, cozening friend, crake a little."

"Can a man not—"

"Not you."

"Put that bow down," Kier mac Aodha said. "Take a

sword—fight us like the man you aren't."

"Now, if a pack of wild dogs run up on you in the dark, do you throw off your bow and plunge in tooth to tooth?"

"Where is your brother?" Dermot said. "I heard he had somewhat of a grudge against us."

"Oh?" Muirtagh leaned up against the stockade wall. "Eager, you are, to have your guts out on the ground."

"And Maelmordha," another voice said. It was red-headed Cormac ó Daugherty, Dermot mac Mahon's foster-brother. "We heard he met your brother in Connaught. We're hunting him."

"Oh, oh, oh, you're running out of bounds again. Had The ó Ruairc found you on his ground, he'd given you a bit less time to talk than I do. Maelmordha's not here. Get out."

"But he was here."

"Yes. He was here. Get out. The ears of you all are marvelous—shall I make some hearing-holes elsewhere in your heads?"

"It's the voices in them that trouble me," Cearbhall said.

Muirtagh's breath sighed out of him. Cearbhall climbed out the loft window and sat, his legs dangling, on the sill. His sword he laid across his knees. "Out of a good sleep they woke me."

The blade of his sword flashed in the sun. Muirtagh lowered his bow. His fingers, warped around the bow and arrowshaft, had been aching for long moments, but he'd not realized it until now. "Well," he said gently, "go on, we are busy men, and our winter something leaner than yours. Save all this frothing for when the Danes come."

Dermot glanced at Cormac, and something passed between them. Dermot turned and rode slowly out the gate. The rest followed. Dermot rode by without saying anything, and Kier mac Aodha started to speak, pinched his lips together, and trotted through the gate.

Cormac drew his horse aside, to stand near Muirtagh, and, glancing back toward Cearbhall, said softly, "Twice now you've been lucky, rabbit. What is it about threes?" He spat at Muirtagh's feet. "Learn to run again, rabbit." Spinning his horse, he loped out after the others.

Cearbhall had disappeared; he emerged again from the loft, climbing down the stair. Muirtagh shut his eyes, feeling sick in his stomach. Cearbhall walked over, swinging his arms, and grinned.

"If that's all they can do in the face of the two of us, we'll live to be old men. What did Cormac say to you?"

"Enough."

"I had to climb in through the back window of the house, fetch my sword, and go up the loft stair without being seen. I thought from the loft I could see more."

"You couldn't use your sword in the loft."

"I was planning to jump down on The mac Mahon. What do you mean, he said enough?"

"They won't let us be."

Maelmordha was at the door, behind Aud, his dark face above her dark hair and pale, staring eyes. Aud called, "Come inside, you two."

Maelmordha said, "I'll go. Thanks, Muirtagh."

Muirtagh shrugged. "It's easy, talking of it when they aren't here. You can't go. They're still out there."

"Where is Eoghan?" Aud said.

"I sent him after the herdsmen."

"How many were there?" Maelmordha asked.

"Ten or twelve," Cearbhall said.

Muirtagh gnawed on his lip. His head was full of ideas all pulling in different directions. "They'll be out there waiting."

He sat down. Niall and Aoir came in, Niall carrying Conall pick-a-back. "Father," he said, "who were they?"

"Your grandfather's murderers' sons."

The children's faces drained as white as Aud's. Cearbhall leaned forward. "Muirtagh—"

"Why not? You chewed at me to say that, to take old Aed's fingerbone to point at them—well, now, look at it. There they are, and they will not let me alone."

Maelmordha said softly, "He's unsettled."

"Unsettled? I'm frightened, that's what I am. Let me think, the batch of you—"

"Father—"

"I said let me think!"

Aud collected the children and led them to the door. "Mama," Niall said. "He shouted at me."

"Go on."

"I'll go the road to Kincora," Muirtagh said. "I'm going to find the King."

"What good can he—" Cearbhall said.

"I don't know. Something."

Maelmordha sighed. "You can't lose the chance, surely. But you could have fenced yourself better against the possibility."

"How? King of Leinster, tell me how."

Maelmordha opened his mouth, thought, shrugged, shut his mouth, and looked away.

Cearbhall said, "It all seems clear to me."

"Living with him ought to have taught you," Maelmordha said. "If there is a crooked way with precipices, and a road on the flat plain, then Muirtagh takes the cliff ride."

"So much for that. I'll go to the King." Muirtagh stood up again.

"I'll go with you," Cearbhall said.

"And Eoghan." Muirtagh pushed his cheeks out of

shape with his fingers. "Who was on sentry duty?"

"One of Brendan's housefolk. He'd gone off for a drink of water."

"Then they've found a place where they can watch the gate clearly enough to see if the sentry's gone. Good. When we go, send Liam out to see how many of them have followed us—they will, I'm sure of it. If none, then Maelmordha can caper out."

The door opened, and Eoghan came in, his bow unstrung in his left hand. "I'm back, Father."

"Where are the herders?"

"Between here and Foinn's stockade. In case—"

He looked around, shy suddenly, and said softly, "In case they might do some better work out there. The mac Mahon's below, on the river, camping. He can't attack both—I mean—"

"Wise head," Maelmordha said.

"Yes." Muirtagh went past Eoghan, toward the door. "Come with me. I have something to tell you."

They went out toward the shed, where the boughs for arrows were aging in casks. Muirtagh stood still a moment, watching Eoghan from the corner of his eye. He wanted to throw his arms around Eoghan, to hold him tight, protect him. He said finally, "I'm going to Kincora in Munster with your uncle, and you can come with us, if you want."

"Kincora?"

"Yes. I want to make some arrows first; don't pack up your extra cloak right now."

"Why not go to Maelsechlainn?" Cearbhall said. "He's closer and he might—"

"You're mad. If he did give us his protection, what would it—he's not just."

"How just is it to shout you're a coward in front of—"

Eoghan whirled. "He's not a coward."

"I said I was frightened," Muirtagh said. "I am." He took a bough out of the nearest cask, sighted along it, and trimmed it with his dagger.

Eoghan settled down, simmering. Cearbhall smiled at him. "That was clever, leaving the men on the hillside."

Eoghan ignored that; he would not be mollified. "You're not a coward."

"Oh, maybe not. But I frighten easily. I'm half woman; my mother was one. Let's make the arrows. They may be of some use, later."

Maelmordha and Cearbhall slept in the one sleeping room, and Muirtagh, the baby and Aud in the other, with the four older children in the loft. Muirtagh lay on the bed, watching Aud tend the baby, and she said, "So. You'll go to the King, and what then?"

She turned the little boy over and dressed him, pulling the shirt down over the fat vigorous arms. Finally, when he didn't answer, she looked at him. "Well?"

"I'll ask him for his protection."

"If he doesn't give it to you, what will . . . happen?"

"I don't know."

"Oh? Strange, when I do."

"You do. With your foresight you might learn the witch's trade."

"I may. There's little enough to do, with the men gone."

"What do you think will happen?"

"How should I know? I'm only an ignorant woman good for nothing but giving you children to rant before and meat to give you the strength to rant before them."

"I'm sorry I shouted at them."

She smiled slightly. "They know it."

"Put him in the cradle."

"You do it."

He took the baby from her, whispered to him to keep him quiet, and carried him to the cradle against the wall. The baby chuckled and sighed when he laid him down. "There, you, go to sleep."

She was in the bed when he went back to it. "Muirtagh, what will you do if . . . if they should . . ."

He lay on his side and put one hand on her shoulder. "Not yet," she said. "Let me ask my question."

He put his arms around her and pulled her tight against him. She shut her eyes.

"Not another woman in Ireland has a man like you. What would I do for comfort, should you turn out like all the rest?"

"Stop talking and you'll have another baby for comfort."

"Oh, yes," she said. She arched her back so that he could draw up her shift. "That's what I need exactly."

In the early morning Muirtagh woke up; before he knew he was awake, he thought, What if they kill Eoghan?"

If I say it it will not happen. If I think of it it will not happen.

He started to pray, to ask God to protect Eoghan, but the feeling he always got when he started to bargain with God overcame him. He lay still, thinking about God; he had always imagined Him as one of the great entwining patterns that the monks made to cage letters in their books, a pattern, but alive in all its parts.

God is in this somewhere. He shut his eyes. If he hunted long enough, traced the thing with his finger, he would find the purpose in it, the clean and honest reason.

When he had been young, before the Flight, there had been a big beech tree in front of his father's house. In the

summer nights, when the woods sang with insects and
the twilight lingered on and on, he and his sister and
some others of the children had loved to sleep under the
beech tree. He lay still, remembering it, the pleasure of
sleeping under the beech tree and not having to decide
what would happen next.

But the beech tree was blasted now, burned and dead;
like a torch it had wavered over the burning houses, the
burning men and women.

"Aud."

She lifted her head. "It's hardly light yet; are you
going already?"

"No."

"You'll want some food to take with you."

"I suppose so."

The baby, hearing her voice, whimpered in the cradle.
She turned her head toward him and the straw rustled.
"Shall I get him?"

"All right."

The first light seeped through the narrow window.
She scurried over to the cradle, snatched up baby and
blanket, and dove back into the bed, snuggling down.
The baby bellowed.

"Sometimes," she said, "when no one's around, I put
him at one end of the bed and I sit at the other end, and
he rolls down toward me."

The baby struggled over onto his stomach and wrig-
gled toward Muirtagh. He got tangled up in his shirt,
fought to get free, and roared. Aud chucked at him. She
pulled arms and legs out of the tangle and, putting her
head down beside his, whispered to him. The baby
cocked his head, listening.

"Aren't you a fine little thing? Yes, you are. Yes, you
are."

The baby gurgled, delighted. Muirtagh sighed. In the

growing, milky light, he watched Aud play with the baby, patting him, tickling him until he shrieked, kissing him. The two faces grew clearer and sharper with the light.

"Muirtagh?" Cearbhall said outside the door.

"I'm coming."

Aud looked up, and like a door her face closed up over the pleasure that had been in it. She got out of bed and dressed while he did, put the baby in the cradle, followed Muirtagh out into the front room, and joined the other women making breakfast.

When they were ready to leave, she gave each of them a sack with bread, cheese and a little jug of usquebaugh in it. Eoghan rode the black pony, and Muirtagh took the chestnut mare, the fastest of his horses. She would be faster, too, now that she was in foal. Cearbhall rode his usual horse, the one he'd taken from Kier mac Aodha. Aud was not at the door when they rode out.

The mac Mahon and his men set off after them at once, seeing that they were going far. Muirtagh held the pace to a quick singlefoot, to cover ground, and the pack behind them made no attempt to close in on them. They rode up the hillside, past the target tree, and headed for the white scar of the waterfall at the high end of the glen.

The mac Mahon's men, unused to riding in hills, started to straggle out into a long loose file. Muirtagh hoped they'd try to find a short way across the bogs, while he and Cearbhall and Eoghan rode from cairn to cairn, but they did not. At the height of the Gap, when Muirtagh looked back, he saw them doggedly following their trail.

"Where?" Cearbhall said.

"Straight west. We go south of the Sliabh Bloom."

They rested awhile at noon, ate some cheese, and moved on. In the midafternoon Muirtagh said, "I should have sent Niall with you to Brefni."

"What?"

"I always meant to have The ó Ruairc foster him, but I never could let him go."

"When we get back."

"And Conall to the church, that I meant, too."

Cearbhall took him by the shoulder and shook him roughly. "When we get back."

They rode on. At sundown, Muirtagh sent Eoghan on ahead to find a suitable place to spend the night. They were already out of the hills, at the edge of the plain. Muirtagh twisted to look back. "Bemused. Maelmordha's safe by now."

"I wanted to ask you: is this for his sake or ours?"

"Both; I am selfish. You know the tale of the man who grazed his goats safely between two packs of wolves?"

"All these old tales. It's a wonder you didn't bring your harp. These two packs aren't enemies."

"Neither were the wolves, that I recall. Here comes Eoghan."

Eoghan galloped up. "There's a rise ahead, with some trees on its top, but none on the slope."

"Is there water?" Cearbhall said.

"At the foot."

"Let's go."

They rode quickly to the hill, filled their waterskins from the spring at the base, and tethered the horses in the grass on the south slope. After they'd eaten, Eoghan and Cearbhall lay down to sleep, and Muirtagh climbed a tree to keep watch, his bow beside him.

The moon was full—he couldn't remember if it had been full the night before or if it was still waxing. The mac Mahon and his men—strange ones, to follow him, a mac Aodha and an ó Daugherty, for all they were foster-brothers—they were all camped off on the next slope, well out of bowshot.

He missed Aud's breathing beside him. He wondered if she slept well when he was gone. He was seldom gone. If he grew so used to her, she might to him. But she could have all the children in to keep her company.

The wind stirred the bare branches of the trees, clacking them together, and he shivered. It wasn't cold. He refused to think of—of Aud and his children, think of— he flung about desperately. The shearing, the calving . . . the murmuring, swarming, all those people screaming, burning, bloody. Aed rearing bloody and naked with his one arm hanging half cut through—no. Think of . . . How they had screamed, and now how they were silent, crowding around him for the warmth of his living body, touching him, trying to get his attention, to tell him something. He was afraid to use his eyes. He knew that their eyes would be sorrowful and earnest and full of something they had to tell him.

"Father?"

Muirtagh collapsed in on himself. "What?"

"I can't sleep."

"Oh. Well, come along up here."

Eoghan clambered up the tree and settled himself into the crook of the branches by Muirtagh's feet. "What were you doing?"

"Saying prayers." He crossed himself against God's wrath. "Your uncle would have me not."

"Did you bring your harp?"

"No. Why?"

"Uncle asked me, I don't know. Tell me a story."

"Oh, God—"

"Oisin. Tell me Oisin."

Finnlaith's favorite story. Muirtagh crossed himself again. Finnlaith would be in that hosting, their serving boy now, until the next died—vast old man, trying to say whatever he had meant to tell the monk. . . . "I can't. I don't have my harp. I'll tell you the Danish story, about the slaying of the dragon Worwrath."

Worwrath was a collection of tales spun together, in some parts not so well, and Muirtagh worked over the rough places, smoothing them in the telling. When he was done, he said, "I'm going to wake your uncle and let him sit watch. I'm tired."

"Can I stay up here?"

"No. You'll be dead tired tomorrow if you do."

They climbed down the tree and woke Cearbhall, who came as quickly and cleanly awake as if he weren't sleeping at all but only had his eyes closed. Muirtagh wrapped himself in blankets and curled up beside the banked fire. With Eoghan and the fire he felt safe from the—them. He went to sleep.

All the next day The mac Mahon and his band were in sight behind them. The day started well, bright and with a fair wind, but after they had stopped to eat and rest their horses at noon, great clouds began crowding up from the southwest. All afternoon the clouds beat their way across the sky. Muirtagh quickened their pace to a lope. The dark swooped down on them and with it the first rain, hard fat drops. Under the horses' hoofs the plain turned immediately to mud.

"Are we going to stop?" Cearbhall said when Muirtagh reined down for a rest.

"No." He stared through the slow rain, looking for The mac Mahon.

"How far are we from Kincora?"

"I don't know. I've never been there."

"This plain may turn to bog."

"I know. Watch for cairns."

He kicked the mare on. Eoghan was tired, the pony

worn out, but they hung on beside the chestnut mare. The rain lessened a little and the wind veered, flying from corner to corner. Muirtagh pushed grimly west, although the mare was beginning to stumble over nothing. They staggered down through a narrow little valley, hemmed and seamed with trees.

"We should stop," Cearbhall said. "The boy's almost finished."

"Leave me," Eoghan said. He struggled up beside them. The pony's head hung; rain dripped from its ears and muzzle. "I'll catch up."

"No."

They rode on a little way, just up the far slope and out of the valley. The wind gusted madly over the plain, driving the rain into their faces. Trees whipped and whirled against the sky all around them. The horses scrambled up a long rise, and when they topped it they looked down at a river and, just beyond it, lights.

"God's Blood," Cearbhall said. "Across all Ireland we could not have reached it so exactly."

"I doubt we did."

They rode down to the river and found that the lights were only fisherman's fires in the low huts on the far bank. The river was flooding into the swampy low ground beside it, and the reeds sang like harps in the wind.

"Who has a rope?" Muirtagh said.

Cearbhall took his from his pack and handed it across. They tied themselves together with it, loosely, Muirtagh in the middle. Cearbhall, whose horse was biggest and strongest, took the upstream side. For a while he couldn't make his horse go into the water. The big horse plunged, heaving back on his hind quarters, snorting. Cearbhall put him at the river again and the horse whirled away, wrapping Cearbhall in the rope. He unwound himself.

Muirtagh pulled off his belt, rode over, and beat the big horse across the flank. The horse snorted, squealed, kicked out, and leapt forward. Muirtagh shouted to Eoghan to warn him. The mare drove after the bigger horse.

All three abreast, they trotted through the swampy ground. Muirtagh could feel the earth sucking at the mare's hoofs. Suddenly there was no bottom. The mare almost sank entirely. The rope around Muirtagh's waist jerked in both directions. He looked for Eoghan—the pony carried no rider.

Muirtagh snatched for his dagger to cut himself loose from Cearbhall so that he could go after Eoghan, but before he could find the slack of the rope he saw a head bobbing just beside the pony's shoulder. Looking hard now, he could see that Eoghan's hands were wrapped in the long black mane, and the pony was swimming steadily.

The current caught the chestnut mare and swung her around. Muirtagh, hanging on while the rope dragged him off, got a mouthful of muddy water. Drowned . . . Cearbhall gave way and he lay across the mare's back, choking. He couldn't see either bank; all he could see was the river, the occasional whitecaps racing over the tossing water.

The mare seemed to falter under him. He took a deep breath. The mare lurched and drove with her hind legs, her hoofs on firm ground, and madly she bolted up the shallow bank. Eoghan she half dragged from the pony's back. Cearbhall's horse hurtled up beside her, snorting and stamping his feet. They waded through the shallow flooded reeds to the high ground.

"Eoghan?"

"I'm all right." His voice sounded stronger than it had before.

"Let's go."

They rode to the fishermen's huts. Muirtagh looked out at the river; already it seemed broader than it had when they'd begun to cross. The whitecaps were like gulls on it.

Cearbhall slid down from his horse and hammered on the nearest hut door. The door opened a crack and a husky voice called, "Who's there?"

"Travelers—The ó Cullinane of the Glen by the Gap. Let us in, we're freezing."

Muirtagh, sitting dumbly on the mare, looked at Eoghan and saw him shivering. He pushed the mare over and threw one arm across Eoghan's shoulders.

"Come in, then," the fisherman said. "Ah, it's a boy. Now, you crossed the river with a boy?"

Muirtagh and Eoghan dismounted at once. Eoghan said, "I'll t-t-tend the ho-ho-horses." His teeth clicked.

"I will," Cearbhall said. "There's an empty shed back there. You go in." Over Eoghan's head he grinned at Muirtagh and reached for the reins. Muirtagh gave Eoghan a gentle shove through the door.

"It's a bad night to be on the highroad," the fisherman said. He stood aside. "Worse still to be in the river."

They all went to stand by the fire. Muirtagh told the fisherman who he was, and the fisherman said, "The Glen by the Gap—where would that be?" He took a blanket from a heap by the wall. "Wrap him in that."

Muirtagh helped Eoghan get off his wet clothes and threw the blanket around him. "Over in the hills southwest of Dublin."

"Oh?"

Muirtagh rubbed Eoghan until the boy's skin was bright red; he himself began to shiver. He slung the blanket over Eoghan's shoulders and sat down on the hearth. "Can anyone cross that river now?"

The fisherman settled down on his heels—there was no furniture in the hut, and the smoke from the fire lay like fog only a few feet from the floor. "You're mad," the fisherman said. "I'd have said nobody could cross the river when you did."

Cearbhall ducked in through the door. He lowered himself down out of the smoke. He alone of the three of them wasn't shivering and blue with cold. "They won't cross tonight," he said.

The fisherman made a palms-up gesture. "The nearest ford's up by the King's Rath—who's chasing a clan chief all across Ireland?"

Cearbhall took one of their jugs of usquebaugh out of his shirt. Muirtagh shrugged. "Another clan chief." He watched Eoghan gulp usquebaugh. Eoghan could scarcely keep his eyes open. Gradually he sank down onto the floor, curled up, and went to sleep.

"Sometimes—" the fisherman said. He stirred up the fire. The hot turf glowed sullenly. "Messengers, all along the river—some curraghs, even. People coming in from all over."

"There's going to be a war," Cearbhall said.

"Oh? Has there ever not been a war?" The fisherman made the palms-up gesture again. "He should never have been King. What is there in his blood of Niall of the Nine Hostages? None. The clans want their own, they want an ó Niall, not a come-up Dal Cais prince for a High King."

Muirtagh took the jug and handed it to the fisherman, who drank deeply. "He's been King a while now. He's done some good, he's done some bad—what King does more or less?"

The fisherman shrugged. "Would your clan take another man for a chief while you were still alive and claimed it? The High King of Ireland is The ó Niall of

Tara. No. This one . . ."

Muirtagh was thawing out slowly, growing sleepy, and he shut his eyes a moment. He heard Cearbhall say, "Let him rest—we came all this way in two days' riding," and he sighed and slumped down and never felt his head touch the floor.

When they woke in the morning the rain had stopped, although the sky was packed full of iron-grey clouds. They took the breakfast the fisherman offered—dried fish and bread—and rode off along the river, headed north. Eoghan was full of talk about the river crossing, which he remembered in every possible detail.

Muitagh could feel his will stiffening. He refused to think about what would happen at Kincora. It was enough to get there. But slowly his mind gathered up all the persuasions, all the old arguments, and because he didn't think them enough he wanted the King's protection so much that he ached from it.

In the forenoon, at last, they saw Kincora across the plain, stirring in the wind that flew under the clouds. Surf boomed on the lough shore behind the hall. Muirtagh looked across the river for The mac Mahon; he'd been doing so all morning.

But now he saw them. They were whipping up tired horses toward the ford. Muirtagh reined in to watch.

"Will he be here?" Cearbhall asked. "The King?"

Muirtagh nodded.

The chestnut mare tossed her head, eager to be going. She was in good condition, and after the night in the shed she was flighty. She pawed at the ground. The mac Mahon and his men were halfway across the ford. Muirtagh whirled the mare and put her into a dead run, straight for the stockade ahead. The mare stretched out flat.

Cearbhall and Eoghan raced after him; Muirtagh took hold of the mare's mane and pulled himself into a deeper seat. They would think he was mad, back there.

Ahead, the stockade gate was open. He aimed the mare for it, not slowing, and saw the sentries rushing about on the walls. The mare gathered herself without hesitating and jumped the ditch just before the gate. Cearbhall and Eoghan veered over to cross by the bridge, and their horses' hoofs drummed on the wood.

Muirtagh shot the mare through the gate, sat back hard, and made her skid to a stiff-legged halt, right in front of King Brian's hall. Cearbhall and Eoghan almost crashed into him. The gates slammed shut.

"Who goes?" a sentry shouted. "Who's after you?"

The front door of the hall flew open. It was beginning to rain, and all the men of the King of Ireland's house were inside carousing. Two warriors with axes came out and added to the shouting. Muirtagh grinned.

"I am The ó Cullinane," he cried. "It's The mac Mahon and some of his people after me."

The two warriors looked at each other. One went back into the hall, and the other came forward to hold Muirtagh's rein.

"Yes," he said. "I remember you from Tara—the harper. Come inside. It's cold."

"Hah," Cearbhall said. "Tell me something useful."

Muirtagh threw one leg across the mare's withers and slid down her side. "My brother and my son are with me." He waited for Eoghan and with him beside him went into the hall.

The old King sat in the high seat, just as he had at Tara, bent, with his beard on his chest. "Well, Muirtagh," he said. "What brings you so precipitously to my hall?"

All the men of the Dal Cais were sitting on the benches, their eyes on Muirtagh, and he looked up and down their ranks before he said, "The mac Mahon, sir."

The old King looked to one side. "Room for The ó Cullinane. Will you sit, Muirtagh?"

Cearbhall came in and the King greeted him. "If you will sit, gentlemen, and eat, I will . . . think on it."

Muirtagh, content, went to where space had been made on a bench and sat down. He took Eoghan on his left and Cearbhall on his right. Servants fed them. Eoghan sat with his hands in his lap, and Muirtagh said, "You say your own thanks in a place like this. They hold with little prayer here." He made the sign of the Cross over his food and cut a slice from the joint of meat.

Eoghan bowed his head a moment, looking from side to side to see if anyone was laughing, signed his dish, and fell to eating. Muirtagh grinned. Cearbhall was already halfway through a small game hen. Down along the benches, men were nudging their neighbors and smiling at Eoghan and Muirtagh.

"We have a priest here to bless," someone said.

"Ah," Muirtagh said. "Then you weren't at Cathair."

The King leaned forward—he was not eating. "Felim, he'll give you a speech to have your head ringing for hours afterwards, if you let him pause in his dinner. Be quiet."

A servant came to the King and the King spoke with him at length. The servant went off through the front door.

Muirtagh grinned. By now, The mac Mahon, waiting outside, would be soaked to the skin in the fresh rain. They must have stayed hard on Muirtagh's trail the night before, for fear of losing them in the storm, and on the barren side of the river their night would have been . . . interesting.

The servant came back in and caught the King's eye and nodded. The King sent him off with a wave of his hand. The white head swung toward Muirtagh, who straightened a little.

"Should it wait?" the King said. "What brings you here, Muirtagh?"

"Better it come out in the open air. I'll speak of it now, if it should please you."

"That I won't know until I've heard it. Speak out."

"Aengus ó Lochain, who was Eolainn's son—fostered by The ó Niall of Ulster under Maelsechlainn—came to me in my stronghold not so long ago and said he came from you, to hear what I meant by the harping at Cathair."

"I never sent him."

"I know. Dermot mac Mahon and Cormac ó Daugherty—Kier mac Aodha, your cousin, maybe—they did. Then only some few days ago Dermot, Cormac and Kier with some others, all young, came to the Glen and spoke carelessly to my wife and gave me to think they meant to open up the feud again."

The King frowned. "Did they leave nicely?"

"My brother and I helped them somewhat. There was no fighting."

The King stood up. "I wish that all but Muirtagh leave this hall."

Everyone rose. Cearbhall said, "Let me stay."

"No. And take the boy." The King's eyes slid over Eoghan.

"Father—"

"Go with your uncle. Now, go on, there's no harm here." He looked at the King. "We are all friends here."

A servant came to Cearbhall to guide him out. The King caught the servant's eye and said, "Fetch me The mac Mahon—no one else."

"No," Cearbhall said.

Muirtagh looked at him and shook his head slightly.

He hadn't expected this, but when he thought of it—quickly, his mind leaping—he thought it might be better.

The hall emptied, and Muirtagh walked around the table to stand in front of it.

"He's a handsome boy, your son," the King said.

Muirtagh cleared off a place on the table and hitched himself up onto it. "He is, he favors my father."

"Your brother, too. Who was your mother?"

"The niece of The ó Houlihan of Hy Kinsella." He paused a moment, wondering if the King were hunting for his friends, and said, "I've no allies, if that's what you mean."

"The ó Houlihan is one of Maelmordha's, though."

"He's fled to the hills himself—how can he help me?"

The mac Mahon stormed into the hall, wrapped in a dry cloak; he left a trail of wet footprints across the floor, and his boots sounded soggy. "Sir—"

"God be with you," the King said.

The mac Mahon noticed Muirtagh and whirled. "By the Holy Cross of God, I'm—"

"Stand still," the King said. "You are in the King's hall —are you so ill-bred in Meath?"

The mac Mahon settled back on his heels. "Your pardon," he muttered.

"Given. Muirtagh tells me that you and some others of your friends came unbidden and bad-mannered to his stronghold."

"We were chasing Maelmordha."

The King glanced at Muirtagh. One corner of his mouth twitched. "And that took you to the ó Cullinanes?"

"He had been there," The mac Mahon said. "He admitted it." He glared at Muirtagh.

Muirtagh's hands were curled around the edge of the table, and he shrugged slightly. "He was there when you were, Dermot."

The mac Mahon swelled, and his face got very red. The King struck one hand down at him to keep him quiet.

"You foster my enemies?"

Muirtagh looked at him straight in the eyes. "He spent one night with me—he came with my brother from Connaught, from The ó Ruairc. You know how The ó Ruairc sits in this, and you might not touch him, but me you can touch, down to the ninth generation—"

"Answer my question."

"Yes. I foster your enemies. I've been fostering them since the war started. You know that, Maelsechlainn told you, back at Cathair. But then you said nothing."

The King paused, too long, and said, "Maelsechlainn said what he suspected. I thought too well of you then to believe him."

"Pfft," Muirtagh said. He looked down at his hands.

"This is a blood feud," The mac Mahon said. "This is his business and mine, Sire. What reason to dirty your hands with the likes of him?"

"Pfft," Muirtagh said again.

"You never swore me an oath, Muirtagh," the King said.

Muirtagh looked up. "The father's word goes for the son, from King to King. You swore me an oath—if you didn't, why the high seat and the name King?"

"Will you let him speak so to the High King of all Ireland?" The mac Mahon cried, but the false horror in his voice cracked in the middle of it.

"God's love," Muirtagh said. "Do you think this a game of hurley, child? You said yourself it is a blood feud—and if a chief can't speak directly to a King over the lives of his people—" He jerked his eyes back to the King. "You know all that touches on this, the oath I swore, their business with us that one time."

"I know it. I don't know what you would have me do."

"Make them leave off. Tell him now, keep away from my door and my fields, my herds and my people. So simple? You can accomplish it in one word. Tell him."

The King sat still as stone. The mac Mahon said angrily, "This is no business—"

"There is no man alive whose grandfather was alive when this feud started," Muirtagh said; he lifted his voice up over The mac Mahon's. "The blood let in this one feud would flood the river up into this hall, King. The Danes haven't killed so many out of Meath, in all the years they've preyed on us, as this one feud has done. I won't have the women of my clan bear children for the sword."

"You're afraid," The mac Mahon said.

Muirtagh glanced at him and back to the King. "You judge it."

The old man stared at him. His head turned toward The mac Mahon. "Leave me."

"No," Muirtagh said. "No. Let him stay here."

The mac Mahon was silent; his eyes were bewildered, and he looked from Muirtagh to the King and back.

"You ask—" the King said.

"I ask you only to be the King." Muirtagh gripped the table's edge so hard his arms grew cramped. "If you do not, Maelsechlainn might as well be King as you. Maelsechlainn could not do this—would not, not for my sake."

"I know."

The King looked to one side, into the empty corner. The mac Mahon said, low, "Who are you to fret a King?" His face was white as salt.

Muirtagh said nothing. He reached behind him and

got a winecup and poured it full from an ewer. The King
sat thinking—it was said he knew all the Brehon law; it
was said he had hungered after the High Seat from the
day he was born. Muirtagh wondered how he could bear
being King. It was raining hard, and the thatch was alive
with it, like mice through straw. Muirtagh drank the
wine and set the cup down.

The King's head swung back, and his eyes fixed on
Muirtagh's. "I cannot do it. You know that. I cannot."

Muirtagh sighed. He shut his eyes a moment. Everything seemed to have fled out of him. He drew on it
again, whatever it was that had driven him to it once, and
opened his eyes. The mac Mahon and the King both
watched him, and their faces were both pale, like water
flowers.

"For you, it were better we had all died in the Flight,"
Muirtagh said. "So that when you come up to it and you
must do something that might ruin you—"

"Might? It would. Could I hold his loyalty if I—" He
jabbed a finger at The mac Mahon. "None of them.
Who would follow a King who meddled in the business
of the chiefs?"

"Meddle? For the love of God, the last blood is on his
hands, not mine."

"No King can—"

"Then you can, No-King. Do you realize what you're
doing? If I leave this hall without your favor, I'm a dead
man. And my sons, my brother, my people—all of us.
They'll drive us to fight and they'll slaughter us."

"Why come to me at all?"

"I thought you were a King, not something the
women hang in the trees to keep the crows out of the
field."

"Don't—"

"Forbear is the word you must use, No-King."

The King lurched to his feet. "I am the King. What are you but a man with so many second thoughts he can't decide between them? When you speak to me, you will keep your speech as simple and gentle as a priest's. 'Forbear.' You forbear, who prays like a woman—or prove that you're otherwise."

Muirtagh looked at The mac Mahon and saw him quivering, ready to jump.

"King," Muirtagh said, "you know that you should do it, or you wouldn't malign me. I'll . . . take your judgment on it." He slid off the table. The mac Mahon quivered, but the King moved his hand and held him back. Muirtagh walked to the door.

He had his hand on the latch when the King said, as if it were torn from his throat, "You take it mildly enough."

"Oh? If I raved a little, and beat my sword—the one I haven't got—against the floor, and perhaps cursed, would I win something? I'll leave you to your feast, King, and him to his hunt. Only, hold him here until I am gone. It's only just to give the deer something of a lead, or where's the sport?"

He went out into the rain. He sent one servant for his horses and another for Cearbhall and Eoghan. In the rain he waited, hitching his cloak a little closer around his throat. The rain stroked him and ran down his face.

His brother came out, with Eoghan hooded and cloaked beside him. "Well?"

"It's all up. We'll have to ride a little, put some country between us and them before it all boils into the fire."

"What did he say?"

"He said he wouldn't do it."

Cearbhall glanced at Eoghan. "Maelmordha and I both warned you."

"So you did. Would you like a present for it, or just a

smile and my warmest thanks?"

Their horses came, and Muirtagh swung up onto the mare's back. Cearbhall said, "We should have gone at them—the only way they know, with swords."

"So we should."

A door opened somewhere, slammed in the wind, and flew open again. Someone cried out a question. The gates were ajar, and Muirtagh trotted out. They rode past the earthworks, across the wooden bridge, and started toward the ford across the river.

The rain blew away and the wind dropped. By sundown they were far enough from Kincora that Muirtagh felt safe in stopping for the night. It was getting colder. Over the fire they built and the last of the cheese and bread, they hardly spoke. Muirtagh thought little, only random memories filling his head.

"Wake up," Cearbhall said gently.

"Oh, I'm awake. What do you want?"

Eoghan looked up at him and smiled. His eyes were steady. Aud's smile, strange on his grandfather's face.

"I have some friends near Dundalk," Cearbhall said. "Fenians."

"It's a pleasure to know a man who has friends."

"What do you think will happen?"

"Some of them will favor cutting us down little by little—killing only the men they think are dangerous. You and me, first. But they'll find all of us dangerous, sooner or later. Some others will say that we all should be blotted out."

The King was right; he had so many second thoughts he couldn't decide. He had always been this way. He wrapped his arms around his knees.

"The Fenians I know would fight for love of me," Cearbhall said. "Not many, but all good fighting men, and they're most of them tired of the wandering life."

Muirtagh said nothing; he rested his cheek on his drawn-up knee and stared.

"Muirtagh, what shall we do?"

"I don't care. Whatever you like."

"Why—" Cearbhall said. "It's . . . why—"

Eoghan said quietly, "Let him alone, Uncle. He's tired."

"But—"

"I know."

"We haven't got the time for him to be tired."

"There's nothing we can do without him," Eoghan said. "Let him rest."

Eoghan stood up and slowly raked over the fire. He and Cearbhall wrapped themselves in blankets; Cearbhall lay down to sleep and Eoghan went out of the firelight to sit sentry duty. Muirtagh sighed.

Once that night he stirred, when Eoghan woke Cearbhall and sent him out to watch. They'd put a blanket over him. His back ached from sleeping sitting up and he lay down with a groan. The next time he opened his eyes, the grey dawn was streaming in under the clouds, and Cearbhall was gone.

He woke Eoghan. "I think he's gone after his friends," he said. "We may as well ride with him as far as the hills."

Eoghan yawned. "He wouldn't have left us unwatched, would he?"

"No. He must have just gone. He knew we'd wake up as soon as it was light."

Muirtagh kicked the fire apart and strapped the chestnut mare's sheepskin on her back. Eoghan was bridling the pony.

"We haven't seen The mac Mahon," Eoghan said.

"I'd rather we did, so we knew where he was."

Eoghan started to mount. Muirtagh said, "Lead him a few steps; he's cranky in the morning, and there's no better way to see if he means to put you in the nearest gorse thicket."

The black pony balked at moving, and when Eoghan mounted, he bucked. Eoghan was warned enough that he could keep his seat. Muirtagh grinned.

"There, you see?"

Eoghan nodded and straightened up. "Oh, yes. I should have thought of that."

So cheerful. It was hard to keep in mind that they were all condemned. Muirtagh led off, following Cearbhall's trail.

"I'm hungry," Eoghan said.

"We'll shoot something on the way."

He kicked the mare into a lope. Cearbhall's tracks led up the slope of the next hill and down the other side— from the length of the horse's strides, he was moving fast. The sun broke through the clouds, weak, wintry light, and the air was harsh.

"Father, I can't keep up."

"I'm sorry."

"You were going very fast."

"I'm sorry. I—"

He looked down at Cearbhall's trail, looked up ahead, and frowned. He jogged forward a little and dismounted.

"What is it?"

"Two strange horses."

Muirtagh crumbled the edge of one of the strange tracks; it was very fresh.

"He met someone?"

"They came after him." Muirtagh vaulted back onto the mare and jerked her head up so hard she reared. When her fore hoofs touched the grass she bolted. Eoghan shouted after him. Something was drumming in his ears, behind his eyes, deep in his head, and, riding, he dropped the rein and strung his bow.

Ahead the trail ran around a stand of beech trees, but he sent the mare straight through them, ducking the branches, his heels in her ribs, the bow laid along her side where it wouldn't catch on anything. The mare stumbled and he hauled her savagely back to her feet and she drove on. They burst out of the trees and she shied. He reined her down.

They were some distance from their horses, The mac Mahon and his friends; they stood in a clump, looking at something on the ground. There were nine of them. When they saw him they separated, looking wary, some turning for their horses. When he jogged forward they all stood still. Muirtagh rode up close enough to see the man lying on the ground. It was Cearbhall, and he was dead.

He let the rein go loose. Behind him, Eoghan shouted, and Muirtagh flung one hand out to keep him back. He looked from Dermot's face to Cormac's to Kier mac Aodha's. Now he could see that two other men lay dead in the grass and that two of the living men held wounds tight to keep them from bleeding.

"Twelve to one?" Muirtagh said. "Don't you think you were outnumbered somewhat?"

He drew out an arrow and nocked it slowly. The mac Mahon started forward and Muirtagh raised the bow. The mac Mahan stopped.

"Oh," he said. "Oh, come on, there's two of us, but the boy has no weapon—perhaps you feel that's too many? Attack me—will you not?"

"There's that law—" The mac Mahon said. "It was Cearbhall Aengus said was—we just wanted him."

"What law?"

"The law against killing harpers."

Muirtagh stared at them. "The law against—is there a law against harpers killing?"

He shot. The arrow, launched from so close, thunked into The mac Mahon's chest and passed almost clear through him. The others charged, and Muirtagh jerked the mare back, loped her off, wheeled, nocked other arrows, and killed two more of them. He swung the mare away when they came closer, and killed three when they fled back to their horses. He raced to Eoghan and snatched up his rein and galloped off, bending out to keep the black pony going. He galloped out into the clear, away from all trees, and snatched the mare down to a halt.

They weren't chasing him. Mounted, they turned their horses south and galloped off.

"Father," Eoghan said. "Father."

Muirtagh charged the mare back to Cearbhall's body. He flung himself down and stood, looking.

"The law against killing harpers," he said. "Oh, God."

"Father, we must get home. They'll be there next."

"No."

His knees were soft, and he clutched the mare's mane to stay on his feet. They had hacked Cearbhall to death. Limb by limb he had died, without shouting for help, or they would have heard. Surely they would have heard.

Eoghan took hold of his arm. Muirtagh shook him roughly off. Moving quietly, with soft words, he caught a loose horse—there were many loose horses now. He led the horse back to the body, stepping around other bodies in the tall grass. By one he paused, and his heart gave a queer little jump. It was Kier mac Aodha, doubled up over an arrow through his chest.

"Father."

He jerked. He moved over to Cearbhall and threw him

across the horse's back. Eoghan got rope from the black pony, and Muirtagh lashed the body to the horse. He stood, staring.

"Here are your arrows," Eoghan said.

Muirtagh took them and went to his mare to case them. There were only four, all smeared with blood. The other two must have come out the back. They could not be drawn out, because of the barbs, when they came out the back.

Eoghan was standing beside Cearbhall when Muirtagh rode back. "Poor uncle," he said.

"Go home," Muirtagh said. "You are The ó Cullinane. I've broken my oath. Go and tell them all. My fancy cloak's in the closet. They'll believe you."

"Where will you go?"

"After them. They've gone to Kincora."

"Will you ever come back?"

"No."

"Where will you go?"

Muirtagh swung the mare south. "Don't let it interest you."

"Father," Eoghan shouted.

Muirtagh caught up the rein of the horse carrying Cearbhall and trotted off. Eoghan shouted to him again. At the top of the rise he slowed a little, thinking to look back and make sure that Eoghan was going home, but he only kicked the mare on and rode harder down the far slope.

All that day he rode. At dusk he frightened a rabbit out of a clump of gorse and shot it and that night cooked it and ate it. He could not sleep. He thought of Eoghan going home without a sword, and for a moment almost stood and mounted and went after him. He settled down again. The dark was close and windy, and he felt the old sensation of being crowded and poked at.

It was so, of course. Now it was Cearbhall who was their servant. Muirtagh could shuck off his name for this world but the next would cling to him. They had tried to warn him. Finnlaith had tried.

Attend me, kinsmen. The others, the men he had killed back there—

Kier mac Aodha. He shut his eyes tight. The pretty boy he had teased and mocked—even Dermot mac Mahon he pitied, suddenly. He was older than they and should have—there had to have been some way out other than dead men in the grass and the bloodstained arrows and Cearbhall chewed to death. Some way better than killing boys.

Before dawn he mounted again and rode on. Shortly after the sun rose he came to the river and turned to follow it north. He passed the fishermen's huts on the far shore and saw the glimmer of a breakfast fire. Curraghs lay beside the huts, turned turtle for the winter. He jogged on.

Some time later he rode into the King's stockade. Servants took the reins of both horses, and he told them to leave them in the yard, but to give the mare some water. Few men were around in the yard, and no one stopped him from entering the King's hall.

The King was holding a court, to judge, and from the men who sat on the bench to the right, Muirtagh knew whom they were judging. He stopped just inside the door and said, "I'm sorry to break into your business, King."

"You break into your own," the King said. "What's this I hear?"

"Oh, only proving what a man I am."

"Kill him," Cormac ó Daugherty said under his breath.

"No man may strike another in the King's hall," Muirtagh said. "I'd quote you more laws but I'm not at my leisure. I take it you're declaring me an un-harper? I came to tell you that I am declining all the rights of my father's heir. I'm an outlaw and an oath-breaker, without a clan or a name."

He smiled at the King. "All my kin are dead men. Kill them for the blood-price, if you can make them bleed."

He turned toward the door.

"Hold him," Cormac said.

"When we have judged him," the King said.

Muirtagh swung around beside the door. "By the way, there's a thing out here I brought you, King. You'd better bury it before it starts to stink." He looked at Cormac. "Twice now I've seen you and not killed you, rabbit. What's that about threes?"

"Bury your own dead," the King said.

Muirtagh flung his head back. "You bury him, King. You killed him."

He stepped outside the door, slammed it shut, and vaulted onto the mare. She bolted through the gate. Sentries cried out to him. He let the mare gallop off and slowed her a safe distance away. At a trot, he headed west, off from the river.

Where he went he hardly cared. The mare carried him west. The clouds blew away in the late afternoon, leaving the sky the color of blue ash. The plain was broken, and the sun was lowering over great headlands: he was near the sea.

He thought, It should matter to me where I'm going.

The mare grazed, walking over the slopes. When the night came, he tethered her and sat down under a tree; if he made a fire it would be seen. His whole body ached from riding. He could feel the long muscles of his back like straps.

What he had said in the King's hall had been stupid and vicious and he wished that he could unsay it. They would probably count it bravado. They had to know that he didn't talk that way, usually. It wouldn't matter to them.

He had mishandled it all. Back there, by the beech grove, he had ruined the one chance he'd ever have to prove that he was right and Cearbhall wrong. The words sounded puny. Nobody was right. He shook his head, trying to settle it; the whole wretchedness of it overcame him.

There were no words for it, no way to talk of it or even think. What could anyone say about it? Cearbhall was dead, not wrong and not right, dead and left for strangers to bury. He, Muirtagh, had killed six other men.

He got up quickly and walked down to the mare. That was all. He could feel, still in his fingers, the way he had drawn back the bow string, the way the bow had flexed; he could see, in his mind, how the men had fallen and how they had looked, dead, but he could say nothing more about it than that he had done it. He mounted the mare and rode on, under the odd, starry sky.

In the first light of dawn he came on a flock of sheep, scattered over a bowl of a glen where nothing but faded heather, gorse and rocks covered the ground. Where there were sheep there might be a stockade; he watched the sky for traces of smoke and saw none. He killed an old ewe and lugged her off into the shelter of a rock outcrop. He made a small fire, using dry wood so that it wouldn't smoke, and broiled strips of meat over it. The fat dripping into the flames made him suddenly very hungry.

He hadn't eaten in a long time. No wonder he was thinking wild. He ate all the meat he was cooking and broiled more.

He had to find someplace to stay, someplace to live, far from where other people lived. He had to have water and food within a short distance and the mare needed graze. Now, he thought, this is sensible. This is the sensible thing to do.

Packing up the rest of the ewe in her skin, he started off through the hills, going almost due north to stay out of the rougher ground: a sheep could live there, but the mare couldn't. Nobody seemed to be chasing him, another thing he ought to have worried about. He'd been mad, the night before. He was lucky he hadn't been captured or killed. That night he slept under a tree, but at least he knew what he was doing.

All the next day he rode north, moving slowly and scouting the country, until something told him he'd gone too far north and he should turn west again. When he thought about it, he realized that he was nearly to The ó Ruairc's stronghold in Brefni.

His heart leapt. He would go to The ó Ruairc. Sitting on the mare at the crest of a slope, he trembled, thinking of a fire in a hearth and a bed.

But in the end he turned west.

In the afternoon he reached the shore of a huge lough and made a camp beside it. Sitting before his fire, he wished he had his harp; he wasn't sleepy, and it would be pleasant to play his harp. The wind came up over the lough, sharp and edged with cold. He should have chosen the summer to get outlawed in.

Finally he got up and went after the mare, who was grazing along the shore. He hadn't tethered her, thinking she wouldn't go far from him, but when he came close to her she lifted her head and moved away. He followed her along the shore, but she wouldn't let him get near her, and eventually he gave up. She put her nose down to the grass and began to browse again.

If she got away from him he was helpless. The thought of being left on foot in this country, of being seen and chased on foot, took the breath out of his lungs. The mare swished her tail across her hocks and flicked an ear at him. He took a slow step toward her and she snorted.

He didn't want to scare her away entirely; he turned and walked back up the shore. The air smelled harsh and wet, as if it might snow. The stars were fading out behind a thin cloud. He looked back and saw the mare following him, but when he stopped she stopped. He went on.

Ahead, the hills came down straight into the lough. The steep slopes would be shelter against the snow, if any came, and he walked faster, tucking his hands inside his shirt to keep them warm.

When he drew nearer the hills he saw a hut alongside the water, right where the slope met the shore. He stopped dead, sniffing, but he smelled no smoke. A little decline ran down toward the hut, rising to the left into a ridge. He angled along it, staying low. When he was close enough to see that the roof of the hut had fallen in, he sat on his heels and thought.

The wind rose and slashed across his face. He plucked a blade of grass and tasted it—tough, but good. Mountain grass. He could fish in the lough. This was a fisherman's hut, abandoned for the winter.

Crouched over, he moved closer. Nothing happened. The place was clearly deserted, and now he could see the grass growing between the stones, the wreck of the thatch. He straightened and walked boldly in.

The hut was full of its roof. He could barely squeeze in. But it had a hearth and the walls were still strong. An old kettle lay on its side near the door, rusted so deep that when he touched it the rim crumbled away under his fingers.

He walked back to his fire under the tree, banked it, and rolled himself up in his blanket. As soon as he put his head down, he slept.

The next morning he nibbled on cold cooked mutton and wondered how he would catch the mare. She was dozing on the lee side of the line of trees and brush of which his tree was part. He looked out at her once or twice, studying her. She was awake enough to flap her ears when he stood up.

He eased softly between his tree and the next, and she looked over at him. He stopped dead. The mare shook herself, snuffled, and stood, her ears pricked up, watching him. He walked quietly toward her, and she didn't move. He took her by the halter and led her back to the fire.

He packed everything—the ewe's remains, mostly—onto the mare and rode her to the hut. The grass in the meadow the ridge and the mountain formed against the lough was actually better than in the open, and, protected, it would grow back sooner in the spring. He walked around the hut, as much as he could. The back wall was the slope of the mountain, and it wasn't much of a hut. Imagining it, back there by the fire, he'd thought it much bigger.

All that day he cleaned it out, piling the old thatch against the side toward the lough. By noon it was snowing, watery and heavy flakes. He found poles in the back of the hut, and even some old turf in one corner. He tilted the poles up from the floor to the top of the wall, braced their bases with stones, and laid the bricks of turf in rows against the poles. The turf wall reached to his head when he stood inside the lean-to.

The snow turned to rain. He stretched his blankets over the turf wall and pinned them fast with splinters. He rode the mare back to the line of trees where he'd slept the night before and cut thick pine boughs. The cold struck through him but he sang on the way back. Inside the hut it was much warmer. While he laced the pine boughs through the top of the log wall, the mare stood in the door, her breath streams of fog. He had to climb up onto the hearth to do the last section of the wall, and while he was up there the mare walked into the hut.

The rain turned to snow again. He cooked the last of the ewe. The mare protested against the fire and he had to bank it before she knocked the new wall down. Her body and his together filled the hut with a sweaty warmth. When he lay down to sleep he hardly needed his cloak.

When he woke up the meadow was glossy with a snow crust. Over the grey sky the sun shone like a ghost, and the wind screamed across the ridge. As soon as he left his door, he began to shiver uncontrollably. He broke enough of the crust that the mare could graze a little. He'd wanted to scout the countryside, but in the snow he'd never get much beyond what he'd already seen.

Instead he took part of his packing rope and unbraided it to make a fishline. The rope was of rawhide, and he'd never heard of a rawhide fishline, but he imagined it would work. He whittled a hook out of sheep's bone.

Toward afternoon, when it had warmed up a little, he struggled down the shore to a place where a stream entered the lough, baited the hook with a scrap of cloth from his shirt, and started fishing. The cold still made him shudder. He was beginning to regret using all his blankets for the lean-to wall. When his hook had sunk to the bottom he reeled it in, unraveled the cloth a little, and cast it out again, higher up the stream.

The fish weren't biting. The cold had probably sent them all to the bottom of the lough. He thought of the fish lying there on the bottom in the mud, their unblinking eyes and the gentle waving of their fins. He got tired of fishing and walked up the shore, looking for crayfish among the rocks. Going back, he cast again and again.

A fish struck, hard, and raced off toward the center of the lough. The wet rawhide stretched like a web. He reeled in, hand over hand, the icy water dripping down his sleeves. The fish tore through the water, jumped, and flopped back again, spraying drops across the surface. Muirtagh reeled madly. Suddenly he met no resistance; he'd lost the fish.

For a moment he only stood, furious, and swore at the fish. Hand over hand, he started to bring in the line. He'd have to undo his shirt—make a linen line.

The rawhide almost tore from his hands. The fish was still there and running. He fought it in until it was splashing in the shallows, got his fingers on it, and tossed it up the bank. The fish flopped across the snow, headed for the stream. Muirtagh snatched for it, missed, got it by the tail, and felt it slither out of his grasp. It was sliding over the snow, away from him, back to the stream. He swore at it and snatched again and again missed, but the fish was done. It lay still, glaring and panting. He reached down to pull the hook out, and the whittled bone slid free at his first touch. He threaded the line through the fish's gills and took it home.

In the days after that, he investigated the land around his hut. Once he saw the smoke of a stockade, well beyond the northernmost edge of the lough, and riding due east, he came on a flock of sheep, left to themselves for the winter in a deep meadow. He shot a sheep and took it home. Fish was boring.

The snow melted away the day after it had come, and almost at once he noticed the first spring buds. The mare liked to eat them and would wander off hunting them if he didn't watch her. He remembered how the ponies in the Glen by the Gap had liked to eat pine-tree shoots.

In the evenings, he carved the frame of a harp from pinewood. It would sound wretched if he ever did manage to string it, but the shape of the harp, the weight and the balance, gave him some pleasure. If he'd had applewood he could have done a good job. The pine was rough to the touch, and he couldn't get the curve of the top properly. The pine grain ran counter to the design of the harp.

He wondered one night what he would do if anyone happened on him. They'd have him trapped. The mare was outside, and he'd made a fire. He put a fresh log into it. If anyone found him, he'd have to kill him. That was what outlaws did.

Aed had never taught him to be an outlaw. No matter what he did, he always managed to be unprepared for it. Even when he tried to do what everybody expected of him, he did it differently.

The mare was just outside the door; he could hear her breathing. If she came in, she'd make him put out his fire. He got up to shoo her away. He stuck his head out the doorway, ready to yell at her, and the words jammed up in his throat: it wasn't the mare but a big monk who stood there, breathing.

For a moment Muirtagh only stared, astonished. It was the monk who had buried Finnlaith. Finally, the man said, "May I come in?"

"Yes. Of course."

"Thank you. I saw your smoke and thought to be warm for once."

Muirtagh backed into the hut so that the monk could get in. The brown cassock stank of wet wool and when the monk sat down he sighed and stuck his bare feet at the fire. His feet looked hard as hoofs.

"Do you want something to eat?" Muirtagh pointed to the mutton on the board he used for a trencher.

"No, thank you. I've already eaten. Are you mad?"

"What?"

"They say you're mad, you've gone completely mad."

"Who's that?" He sat on his heels and wrapped the meat in a bit of hide.

The monk shrugged. "The people I see. Would you be interested in the news? All the—everybody—how long have you been here?"

"Oh." He tried to think. "Since it snowed. Do you remember when it snowed?"

"Certainly, I felt it hard enough. The Danes are to come to Dublin by Palm Sunday. That's the news."

"Oh. The war. Has anybody done anything—Maelmordha, I mean?"

"No. Nobody knows where Maelmordha is. Do you want to know how they've judged you?"

"I can imagine that." He thought of his clan, left open

to The mac Mahon, whichever the new one was, and shrugged that off. "Did they bury my brother properly?"

"Very properly. They had a bishop in to say the proper things. He's a hero, all the songs are very current."

"Palm Sunday."

It all sounded far away and unimportant, all of it. He shook his head.

"They've said you're mad, as I told you," the monk said. "The King thinks you're pure Suibhne, and there's no price to be paid for your killing. No one's out hunting you, odd as it sounds. The ó Cullinane is free of any charge against you, because you're mad."

"Who said that? The King?"

"That you're mad? He—"

"I mean that The ó Cullinane should be free of blame for me."

"Yes, the King."

"Why, the—what a wicked mind that is, there."

"I heard you asked him for something of the sort."

"Twice, but the first time I hardly offered him an ending quite this tidy."

The monk was warming each toe separately at the fire. "This is very snug."

"It serves. Outlawry's not so bitter as we're told. It's only that I don't know what to do."

The monk smiled. "There's no school where you can go to learn it."

"The neglect of it's a scandal. Send to Clonmacnois, tell them they must widen the cursus—put outlawry next to Latin."

He put his head down a little. "I'm too old to be doing this."

"Why don't you go to a monastery? They couldn't

touch you there."

"That's a tempting idea. But I've heard tempting is sinful." He brushed his hair back out of his eyes. "I'll go . . . to Maelmordha."

"Why?"

"I don't know. I think . . . I think I died, back there beside my brother, but I don't know it and nobody else does, but if I go back I'll find my corpse and I can slip back inside it."

The monk stared at him a moment. "You weren't killed at Dublin."

"No, I—"

He lifted his head and laughed. "I'm not mad, really I'm not."

The monk shrugged. "God directs all things to their proper end. Why go to Dublin?"

"I owe the King something. Why should I let him give me outlawed what he wouldn't give me when I was a chief?"

"Vengeance is foul."

The monk's voice was harder than before. Muirtagh looked at him, seeing the dark eyes angry.

"It's not vengeance, really. Or maybe it is. The blood's there, on the ground, and he's pretending it isn't."

"You killed over it once."

"It doesn't seem to have made much of an impression, somehow. Nothing I do seems to." He took his head between his hands. "They aren't even hunting me, you said."

"It's common pride, then."

"No. No. And it isn't vengeance, either. Don't you see?"

The monk watched him. "I suppose I do. But I shouldn't like being you, if you . . . feel that way."

"How do you think I feel?"

"You want to make the world reel because you're alive."

"That isn't it at all."

"If not, what is it? It's a childish thing to want and—"

Muirtagh whirled around, still sitting, and said, "I don't want that."

"Then tell me what it is."

"I—" He fought through it. He did want them to know that he was there, that he had done something that by all rights he should be dead for, but beyond that lay another thing. "I don't know, exactly."

"Going to Dublin will prove nothing. What can you learn among Danes and pirates?"

"Maybe I can find out why being Irish killed my brother and made me kill—"

"Being Irish has nothing to do with it. You're a man, a Christian—"

"No. Be quiet, will you? I can't think straight any more—I don't know what I've got to do—that wasn't the end of it, back there. If I don't go back—don't you see? If I let the King get away with it—"

The monk sighed. "Can't you leave it to God?"

"No!"

The monk crossed himself and began to pray. Muirtagh felt the tension drain away from him; he listened, crossing himself when the monk did, and the words sank gently into him. He listened until he was so tired he couldn't stay awake. He slid down and curled up by the fire. He shut his eyes.

The monk's voice said, "There are certain things that aren't to be known," and the monk lay down and went to sleep too.

In the morning when he woke up, the monk had gone. Muirtagh ate some cold meat, stirred up the fire, and sat near to it to keep warm. The uncertain warm weather of the first spring was changing to a deep cold, deep as the bone.

The chestnut mare ambled into the hut, almost squashed Muirtagh, and put up her customary protest about the fire. Muirtagh patted her. Her tail was so long it might have caught fire anyway.

All day long he sat there, staring at the fire, thinking. Once, when his rump began to itch from sitting too long, he walked to the shore and back. Most of the day he only thought. When the twilight crept in through the door he was tired of thinking, and he still didn't know any more about it than he had when he rode out of Kincora outlawed.

In the old songs there was art to everything, and he thought that was what he missed about this. He gave up thinking and slept. In the next dawn it was still blistering cold, and he assembled all his gear so that he could leave.

He'd picked up far more than he'd noticed in the short while he'd been in the hut: sheepskins, a number of hooks and awls of bone, the pinewood harp, odds and ends like platters and the cooking frame. He left all but the sheepskins and the hooks and awls in the hut. He mounted the mare and rode east.

By noon he realized that it wasn't so easy to ride to Dublin. He had some meat with him, so he wasn't hungry, but the cold was seeping into him like a disease. Even with all the sheepskins around him, he couldn't keep warm. It wasn't even the cold so much as it was the dampness. Everything seemed soaking wet.

When he stopped for the night, he was surprised to find how much of his meat he'd eaten. Over half of it was gone. He huddled by the fire and tried to figure out how far it was to Dublin. His food wasn't going to last that long.

Waking up the next morning was hard; he wanted to lie asleep, close to the fire, not stand up and put his head into the cold wet air and go off riding. He had to force himself to rise. When he was mounted, he rode grimly on, headed due east, but he rode slowly, letting the mare graze.

Toward noon he saw smoke ahead, a smudge over the horizon, and he swung the mare north to avoid it. He sent the mare along the sides of slopes, not over them, so that he wouldn't be silhouetted against the sky; from one slope he looked north and saw two men, on foot, far down the moor. One flung out his arm toward him. Muirtagh kicked the mare into a trot down the hill.

He was afraid to stop that night. His food was all gone now. He stayed on the mare, pushing her along just enough that she didn't stop entirely. If he stopped and built a fire, he knew he would never leave it. Was it better to die warm of hunger or to die hungry of cold? If he made a fire it would be the end of him. When the mare tried to stop he beat her on.

The sun came up over the edge of the far hills, glittering with frost, cold-locked. They looked a little like his own hills, a fortress wall. But they were strange to him. He saw too many signs of other men that day, and forced the mare on toward the hills.

Once he dozed. When he woke, the mare had stopped still and was asleep, her hip cocked. He straightened slowly, easing his cramped, cold muscles. They were at the edge of a wood, and deeper in the wood he could hear the ringing of axes on trees. He woke the mare and when she protested he lashed her with his belt until she moved.

That night, in the hills, he gave the mare her head. She took him straight to water. His teeth rang like bells, clacking together so hard his jaw ached. The cold had taken root in his marrow. He dismounted to break the ice on the pond with his heel, and his feet struck the ground so hard—cold ground, numb feet—that he thought they'd broken off at the ankles. He could barely walk.

Without his willing it, his hands gathered up dead branches and chips of bark and got flint from his pack. He lit the fire and curled up around it. When the sun reached the top of that tree, he would leave. Just until the sun reached the top of that tree . . .

The mare snorted and he climbed out of sleep; it was like being at the bottom of a sun-warmed lake and fighting to get to the surface. It was better to stay in the water, better to lie still and stay in the warm . . .

He opened his eyes and saw wolves sitting in a circle around him. The mare was standing almost in the fire.

Muirtagh drew a long breath. The air was so cold his lungs wouldn't take much of it in. The wolves were skeletons covered with fur—like the hills where his hut had been, the rock showing through the heather, these wolves with their bones knobbed under their pelts. There were four of them, and they were scarred and looked sick and were surely dying. He lurched to his feet. They scurried away, reluctant to leave their meat even if it was still alive.

He took his bow and strung it, moving slowly, and took an arrow from the case. The wolves were watching him with narrowed eyes. He lifted the bow and shot.

One of the wolves yelped, pitched into the air, and thudded to the ground. The other three howled. They raced off, but, still in bowshot, turned and sat down, their tongues hanging out.

Muirtagh walked slowly to the dead wolf; the smell of blood made him reel. The wolf wasn't dead and he had to shoot it again. He dragged it to the fire, laid his bow down, and with his dagger slit the wolf's belly. The other wolves were sneaking in, creeping along on their bellies, pretending to be still when he looked up. He thrust one hand into the wolf's ribcage and jerked out the heart, cut it to pieces, and ate it. His stomach churned violently but he kept it down.

He ate the wolf's liver, skinned the carcass halfway out, and cut what meat he could from the shrunken quarters and ribs. The bloody handful he cooked over the fire. When he had eaten the rank meat, he slung the carcass out to the other wolves, but they shrank from it and would not go near it.

The wolves had made the same mistake he had: they'd stayed where it was safe, in the high country. They lay still, their heads on their paws, their eyes shifting from him to the mare, bound to eat him or die.

His stomach felt unwell, but the meat was enough to keep him on his feet. He caught the mare. She was in better condition than either Muirtagh or the wolves, and she bucked when he mounted. The wolves stood up. He waved his bow at them and started off, with the wolves following as dutifully as servants.

He rode steadily down toward the plain, with the wolves in single file behind. Once they charged after him, but the mare loped easily away, and they stopped almost at once. Just after noon he crossed a dry stream bed at the edge of the plain and the wolves turned abruptly back. He sat the mare and watched them jog up the hill. He hoped they caught something—mice, maybe a stray cow. They topped the hill and jogged along it for a while before they disappeared over the crest. That afternoon, the cold broke.

He rode through pastureland, sleeping by day, hunting at night. Two nights he waited beside a cattle herd for a chance to cut out a calf. He shot several rabbits in that time but the lean meat didn't satisfy him. He'd heard of people starving to death when they had plenty of rabbit meat. He needed fat.

Finally a gawky little heifer wandered over to the edge of the herd. He approached her cautiously, wanting to get in a close shot so he'd have time to hack off some of the meat before the other cows brought the herders down on him with their ruckus. The heifer saw him and came toward him. She was as tame as a dog. When he led her away from the herd she went obediently; he supposed she had lost her mother young and been raised out of a bucket. He took her off a good distance, killed her, butchered her, and ate beef until he was sick.

He packed up as much of the heifer as he could. The herders would be sure to see that she was missing. Still riding by night, he started off for Dublin again. The night after he'd killed the heifer, he rode into the foothills and came upon a huge stockade, with a ditch and an earthworks—some big clan's stronghold. He sat a moment, sniffing the turf smoke and watching. Any clan chief would know Muirtagh the Bowman; he did not go in to chat and sit by the warm fire.

The nearer he came to his own country the uneasier he got. He didn't want to come across anyone he knew. He began recognizing moors and hills he rode over, even at night.

Once he thought he heard someone shout his name. He jerked the mare to a halt and looked all around. Sweat popped out all over him. The wind flew down over him and chilled him. But he saw nobody and heard nothing more, and, pushing his hair back over his eyes, he rode on.

He thought of sneaking in for his harp, but when he began to plan how he would do it he saw how ridiculous the whole idea was. His palms itched for the smooth applewood, and now and then strains of music rang in his mind, unbidden. His ears strained, listening for the voice that had called his name.

At last he turned and rode due north, deep into Meath, to get away. The thought of the deep glens, the trees all green with moss and in the heat of noon dim as twilight, filled him with hopelessness. He thought of Aud and his children. Whatever she thought of him now, it couldn't be good. The farther he got from his own country, the easier this riding became, and finally he turned east and could shrug it off.

The thaw was coming—the ground was looser, the buds pale on the trees. He wondered if the elders were advising Eoghan, telling him how to put seed into the fields, when, which to leave fallow, which to bring back, where to put the sheep and the cattle, which mares to breed and to what stallion—it was a difficult thing. He remembered how he'd hated being the chief, back when he'd been a boy and new to it.

He had come too far north. During the days, when he was camped, he saw some other men, and he could tell by their clothes that he was almost to Ulster. Going east was harder now. This part of Meath was full of stockades and herds and fields, and he had to go slowly, pick his way along, avoiding them all.

One morning, when he stopped to rest, it began to rain —the soft misty spring rain. The planting rain. He rolled himself up in his blankets, pulled them over his head, and slept, and when in the late afternoon he woke the blankets were soaked through. He caught the mare and rode on, safe in the rain. He hadn't gone more than a few miles when he rode in between two hills and came out smack against the sea.

The wind struck him like a blow—tears sprang to his eyes. The surf was white against the pale sand, and beyond the surf the sea ran grey and rolling, whitecapped and full of spray. Not even a gull flew out over it—they were all nesting in the sand, among the bleached drift- wood and the weed at the high-tide line. The crash and roar of the surf lay under the shriek of the wind.

He stared at it numbly. He had never seen the sea be- fore. He'd always imagined it a great lough. But this was . . . He quivered. Out there, past the horizon invisible in the rain, was another country, and beyond that, an- other, and so on, out to the islands Brendan had found. All his life he'd thought Ireland all there was to the world—

There was something out there. He squinted. The mare's head was up, and her ears pricked forward; she'd seen it too. The rain hid it.

Somewhere very close a bell began to ring, and he jumped. He whirled the mare and galloped her along the sand, away from the bell. Up there, the thing on the sea swayed in toward the coast, lumbering through the waves. He reined the mare down hard. The bell—yes. It was a Danish ship out there. He could see the mast.

The wind would force it in, and it would break up on the shore. He trembled, watching. The ship wallowed in toward him. It wasn't moving as fast as it should, in this wind. He couldn't see if there were oars out.

Halfdan had told him about those ships, with a queer passion in his voice. Then Muirtagh had thought him a little mad to want to lurch around the sea in a boat when he could live quietly in a house on the land. A boat like that might take him to Tir-na-nOg. Anywhere.

He trotted along the shore, keeping level with the ship. It never came in close enough that he could see it in de- tail, and finally it swerved out to sea and vanished in the rain. Muirtagh sighed and rode south.

He forgot the boat almost immediately; there were

riders all around. He thought he was close to Dublin. He had some trouble keeping away from the horsemen; often he had to stop and wait in the hills by the sea until men in clanking mail shirts jogged by or some rider on a small swift horse galloped over the horizon. So much bustle fit the notion he had of a town getting ready to fight, but it made it harder for him. All that night he swerved to avoid fires.

Just before dawn, he sighted the tower, on the far side of the river. He rode west a little way until he came to a ford, crossed over, and immediately had to hide in a grove of trees while a little flock of sheep trotted past, toward the town, with two Irishmen driving them and gossiping. When they had gone over the next hill he rode a wide circle around them and came, finally, up to the wall around Dublin.

He sat the mare a moment, watching the wall—there were sentries on it. They saw him and pointed, and one shouted, "Who goes?"

"I'm looking for the King of Leinster."

"Who are you?"

Muirtagh's shoulders twitched. It was none of their business. "Tell him the harper from Cathair."

"We'll fetch him. Don't move."

"Don't move," Muirtagh said to the mare. "Don't move, he tells me."

He looked behind him to make sure nobody was coming, and slid down to the ground. He sat crosslegged in front of the mare. The sun was out, and it cast his shadow across the dust. His shadow looked odd; he put his hand to his face and realized that he had a beard like a pagan Dane's, growing in all directions, and his hair was hanging in his eyes. He reached up to brush it back and the gesture was familiar. He shrugged.

"Muirtagh!"

That was Maelmordha. Muirtagh rose and vaulted onto the mare and rode toward the gate. Maelmordha was on the wall.

"God's Blood, it is you. Come in. You look like a madman."

"They say I am, I hear."

He trotted through the gate, and Maelmordha came down the stair, grinning.

"They say?" He slapped Muirtagh on the knee. "Everybody's seen you at least thirty times since you walked out of Kincora—according to the most reliable people you've killed fifty men. Where have you been?"

"Coming over from Connaught."

"Before then. What happened to you after the killing?"

"I started coming over from Connaught."

"How often? And how did you get here without being captured?"

"I rode."

Maelmordha glanced around at the other men standing there. Muirtagh hadn't realized there were so many crowding around. "You didn't see any riders?" Maelmordha said.

Muirtagh shrugged, uncomfortable, and brushed back his hair. "A few." All the men around made him hunch his shoulders.

Maelmordha looked irritated. "They're supposed to stop all they see."

"They didn't see me."

One of the men around them said suddenly, "Is this the man you've been waiting for, King?"

"Muirtagh the Bowman," Maelmordha said. "The chief of the ó Cullinane clan."

"I'm not," Muirtagh said. He dismounted and stood close to the mare.

"Hunh," the Dane said. He was a husky man, and his Irish was thickly accented. "My youngest son's bigger than this one."

"Your youngest son's bigger than Bjorn, too," Maelmordha said. Everybody laughed nervously. "Come on, Muirtagh."

Muirtagh followed him, keeping close to the mare, who was beginning to kick out at the pack of men. Maelmordha slowed so that Muirtagh could catch up. "That big man is Tryggve Sweynson, Tryggve the White, from Iceland. There are many heroes here."

"Heroes," Muirtagh said.

"You're odd. If I didn't know you better I'd say you were mad."

"Since I left Kincora I haven't seen many people. Only one I spoke to."

"Well, come and let someone trim your beard."

They walked up the hill to the stone fort. The town was crowded. Maelmordha saluted several men, calling out to them by name. "We're all to be here by Palm Sunday, and not everybody's come yet. I've heard that the High King will try to get here before then—it may be hard after that. That's why we have the riders out."

Muirtagh put his hand to his beard, curiously. "It was cold, this winter."

"Oh? It wasn't bad here."

A servant took the mare, and she kicked and fought wildly until Muirtagh went up to her and calmed her down. The servant led her off quietly enough after that. Muirtagh and Maelmordha went into the stone fort.

In the hall, several men were sitting around, surrounded by a litter of robes, clothes and gear. They were all Danes, and Muirtagh hesitated a little before walking after Maelmordha. He remembered the ship he had seen.

"Do you have any arrows?" he said.

"Of course," Maelmordha said. "Why ask?"

"Danes always remind me of arrows."

One of the men looked up. He was sitting in the midst of the others, on a black bearskin robe. He was no bigger than Muirtagh, and as dark, and on the back of his head sat a silver-gilt crown. In the ruck of the heavy black fur he looked like a wizard. By the crown and the bearsark, Muirtagh guessed who he was, and anyhow Maelmordha had mentioned his name.

The Dane held his gaze steadily until Muirtagh, walking, almost stumbled, and the Dane looked away, laughing. Muirtagh went after Maelmordha into a sleeping room.

"This came for you some while ago," Malemordha said.

He pushed aside a tangle of clothes on the table and picked up Muirtagh's harp. He held it out, and Muirtagh ran his hands once over his tunic and took the harp. He pulled the cover off. The harp was out of tune, and he sat down to tune it.

"Who sent it?"

Maelmordha got some wine and poured it. "It came by a man who said that you would know by what it was."

"He said more than that."

Maelmordha shrugged. "Here. He said it was from The ó Cullinane."

"No more?"

"That he wished you well."

"Who, The ó Cullinane or the man who brought the harp?"

"Them both, I think."

Muirtagh drank some of the wine and worked on the harp.

"How did he know you'd come here?"

Muirtagh looked up. "Who knows? Being a chief is so

harsh, maybe God gives us certain special knowledge when we come to it."

He put the harp down and rested both forearms on the table. "Was that Bjorn Wolfbrother out there in the hall?"

"Yes."

"It's a great war, if it calls the likes of him up out of the sea. I'd thought him dead."

"So had we all. He sailed out from the Faroes just after the autumn equinox the year before last. He never came back, and so everyone thought he was dead, and not a few of us were relieved over that. My nephew, Sygtrygg, has had some bad dealings with him. But here he is, smiling the same way, all that sweet innocence in his eyes, and he says he went ahunting Vinland the Good but didn't find it. Found something else instead, left, went back again, and couldn't find it."

Muirtagh picked up the harp and ran his hands over the curves, smiling. "Not a thing beyond these Danes, to misplace an entire island."

"He swears it disappeared into the sea."

"Of course. Let them lose a piece of ground and they'll put hand on all the Bibles between here and Miklagard to prove it's an act of God."

"I'm glad you've got your tongue back again, but don't say things like that so loud. He's a very devil, damn him. He'll tell you a lie so you'll say it's a lie and he can kill you for calling him a liar."

"Love thy fellow man."

"It's in his blood, he can't really help it, I suppose. His brother Einar Bjornson—he was named for his father, Bjorn, I mean, while his father was still alive, which may have something to do with it—anyway, Einar's not here, thank God for that. They call him the Bloodletter. You know what that means. There are Danekillers by the double handful in Ireland, but they called your brother the Danekiller and that was a compliment hard-won."

"Oh, but there's a curse in it, somewhere. Worse, that no Dane killed him."

Maelmordha said, "I'm sorry about that. I rather liked him."

"Oh, I was fond enough of him, you know. I raised him. When he was a little boy he used to follow me around and ask me the oddest questions. When he came back after he was the Danekiller it took me a while to recognize him again. But he was an honest man, Cearbhall, and it wasn't just, what they did to him."

The quiet wasn't like the quiet of being alone.

"Is that why you came here?"

"Yes." He drank more of the wine. "What I did isn't enough. And it was only part of a feud, anyway, so they could excuse it. But this is another thing." He nodded. "This is different. I'm going to make them know how rotten it was." He set the cup down. "How rotten it was."

"Well, you hurt them."

"I don't want to talk about it."

"Bjorn spoke of it with a certain admiration."

"Tell him not to. If he does, I'll put him in a song and sing it from sea to sea in Ireland."

Maelmordha smiled. "Well, come along and I'll have one of the women attack that beard for you. And you need new clothes."

"So. Never again will I listen to songs of outlaws properly fed and clothed. And the wine—I've not drunk anything but clear water for so long it's making me odd in the head."

When his beard had been shaven off and his hair cut, he slept. Maelmordha woke him at dusk and they went into the hall to have dinner. All the men were gathered up at the tables, and the small dark man with the silver-gilt crown was talking. All the others were listening, straining as if each word held the measure of their salvation. Muirtagh climbed over the bench and sat down, some eight or ten men from Bjorn, and on the other side of the table. He blessed his meat and leaned back to let a servant pour him mead. Without the beard and the excess hair he felt lighter and very clean.

Bjorn was speaking the mix of Irish and Danish they spoke in the Southern Isles, where he had been raised. Muirtagh listened for a while, until he realized that Bjorn was talking so that the others had to listen and show him how afraid of him they were. Muirtagh began to eat. Almost at once, Bjorn stopped speaking.

Maelmordha talked to several of the men at the head of the table, mostly about the warriors coming to Dublin, who they were, where they were from, and what was to be expected of them. "The High King will bring up the Dal Cais, maybe some others."

"What of Maelsechlainn?" said a man in a silver-fox cloak.

"Maelsechlainn's a running Conchubar," Maelmordha said. "I don't know what he'll do. Muirtagh there knows him better than most. What do you say, Muirtagh?"

Muirtagh jerked his head up and thought. He remembered Maelsechlainn at Cathair. "He'll come. Maybe he won't fight, but he'll bring an army up."

The man in the silver-fox cloak said, "Why do you think he might not fight?"

Muirtagh glared at Malemordha for asking him a question. "He'll wait, maybe. See which of us wins, and have a fresh army to fight the winner with."

"Why should he do that? If the Irish win—"

"He wants his high seat back," Muirtagh said. "If the High King wins, Maelsechlainn will—But maybe he'll fight with the High King against us. I don't know."

"You're Muirtagh ó Cullinane."

Muirtagh nodded and put meat in his mouth.

A redheaded Dane said, "Cearbhall the Danekiller's brother?"

Muirtagh nodded again.

"I've heard," Bjorn said quietly, "that you're something of a harper."

Muirtagh looked up, straight into Bjorn's flat dark eyes. Bjorn smiled and wiped his mouth on one long hand.

"Bjorn," Maelmordha said. "This man is a guest in my hall."

"So we all are."

"What's this?" Muirtagh said. "I'm a harper, Dane. Are you given to killing harpers?"

Bjorn smiled again. "It's bad luck to kill a harper."

"Twice so far," the man next to Muirtagh said, "he's killed men for lying who said they were harpers. He said they weren't harpers at all."

"Hush," Bjorn said. "He says he's a harper. Don't frighten him or his hands will shake."

Muirtagh lifted one hand and looked at it. The fingers were quivering. Bjorn laughed. Muirtagh said, "Do you want a stave from me, you'll have it." He leaned back and called over a servant. "Go fetch me my harp. It's in my baggage. There are two stringed instruments there, bring them both, and the picks to play the other with."

Bjorn leaned back. "You speak like a harper."

"So. I'm a speaking harper, I don't sing."

Maelmordha said, "Bjorn, this one you shall not touch."

Bjorn turned his head a little, enough that he could see Maelmordha through the corner of his eye, and smiled and looked back at Muirtagh. Muirtagh thought of the stories about this one, of all the murders and raids and long voyages; he thought Bjorn must be sick to death of living up to his reputation, and he felt sorry for him.

He got up, feeling a little unsteady in the knees, and went to the door into the little front room and opened it. Two servants were sitting in there, dicing. Muirtagh went through and bolted the door into the yard.

"Don't let anyone come through here," he said to them, "until you can hear a harp in the great hall. And don't stand in front of the door yourselves."

"Is Bjorn there?" one of the servants said.

"Yes. You may cart dead meat out soon enough." He lit a lantern, hung it on the door out into the yard, and went back into the great hall. That door he shut, leaving the little peephole open. The peephole was as long as his hand and a little wider. He thought the distance back to the head of the table was about fifty paces; he counted to make sure. The servant was there, with his harp and the bow.

"Peace to all here," Muirtagh said. He looked around. Bjorn was sitting with both hands on the table. His crown was on the back of his head, but he wasn't smiling any more. The others were sitting motionless. Muirtagh was surprised at his own calm. His knees were still weak, but that was all. He strung the bow and looked down at the door. The lantern light in the room beyond picked out the peephole. He chose an arrow, lifted the bow, and shot quickly, before his hands began to tremble. He lowered the bow and unstrung it.

The men all around the table were on their feet, staring down at the door. One of them swore under his
breath. "He shot it through the latch hole."

"The peephole," Muirtagh said. "The latch hole's too
small for the arrowhead."

He picked up the harp and went to the high seat and
sat down beside it, his bow across his knees. "Bjorn, will
you have my stave now?"

The others began to laugh and beat their hands on the
table. Bjorn smiled, not the mere stretching of his lips,
but a smile like a small child's.

"I'm a bit larger than a peephole," he said. "If you
harp as well as you play the other instrument, there's no
need for the trickwork."

"Well spoken," the man in the silver fox said.

"I haven't played the harp since—since my brother
was murdered. I've no desire to die for being out of practice."

He played a phrase on the harp, tuned up one string,
and said, "Do you have a favorite song, any of you?"

"Play what you like best," Bjorn said.

"Then here's a tale out of Cuchulain's childhood—
rather, three tales, and the first one Fergus tells."

The first was the easiest of the three. It said how Cuchulain came to Emain Macha in Ulster and defeated the
thrice fifty boys of Conchubar's boy-corps at their
games, when Cuchulain was only seven years old. The
music that went for the hurling games he liked best.
Now and then he spoke one line or another, so that they
would hear what was said in the music.

The second tale was more difficult. "This is Cormac
Corlonges' tale." Conchubar had gone to the house of
the smith Culain and sent for Cuchulain to meet him
there. Part of the music was like a crackling fire; that

reminded him of Aud, and for a moment he almost faltered. "But Cuchulain goes unwarned of the smith's ban-
dog that guards his property." The boy came to the
smith's house and the dog attacked him—the harp's
growls and sharp baying made at least one Dane jump.
But the little boy killed the monster, and in payment to
the smith, he became the smith's ban-dog until another
could be found. "So he was called Cuchulain, the Hound
of Culain."

"I can't believe you are out of practice," Maelmordha
said. "I've never heard you play so well."

"Don't interrupt," Muirtagh said. "This is Fiacha mac
Firaba's tale."

Cuchulain became a warrior and rode off with Iubar
the charioteer to the stronghold of the sons of Nachtan,
of whom it was said that the number of Ulsterman now
alive exceeded not the number of those fallen by their
hands.

The first of the fights was easy enough, but the second
took timing; he had to pay close attention to keep his
following fingers from running into each other. He felt
the most difficult part coming up, and his stomach tensed,
but for the first time in his life he got through it without
jamming a string. The third fight was no trouble, but the
whole of the music was so wonderful—the range and the
combatting tones—that he got caught up in it and forgot
to speak any of the lines. At the end the high clear voice
of the boy Cuchulain rose up like a bird winging straight
into the sun, rose up above all the rest of the music and
hung there until the lower voice had subsided and died,
and when he looked at the Danes, he saw how their faces
glowed with it.

He laid the harp down on his knees and reached for a
cup of wine. For a moment, no one spoke or moved, and

at last Bjorn turned to the man in the silver-fox cloak and said, "I can see now why you want to be the King of the Irish, Brodir."

"Are you hungry?" Maelmordha said.

Muirtagh shook his head. He put the winecup down, motioned to a servant to fill it, and set the harp on its foot again. The men in the hall were talking, and under their racket he played the songs he used for practice. They were eating, too, and tossing the bones onto the floor for the dogs, who fought over them. Maelmordha leaned over and indicated he wanted to talk to Muirtagh when he was through.

"Yes?" Muirtagh let the harp ramble on aimlessly.

"You must have had a harp with you."

"No. There are many things that you do better after you've left them a while entirely."

"Did you mean that about Maelsechlainn?"

Muirtagh struck three sharp notes out of the harp, like high-pitched laughter. "Yes."

"I think the Kings think more of us are coming than there will be."

"That's another reason."

Bjorn was growing increasingly angry at something; now he lurched forward and struck a man across the table from him. "Shut up. I want to hear the harper."

The hall fell silent immediately. Bjorn settled back, glaring around him. He wheeled toward Muirtagh and called, "Play something."

Muirtagh cocked his eyebrows at him. Maelmordha bent forward. "Show me what you did at Cathair."

"God. Do you want the blood out of my veins?"

He stopped to drink more wine, wiped his mouth, and grinned at Bjorn. He played Sidhe-music, the songs of the Hosting, with all the sobbing notes and the shrieks like wind through the eaves. One of the Danes near him shivered. A Leinsterman down the table somewhat, who obviously knew what the music was, called out, "Lord God, are you trying to curse us?"

Some of the Danes began to babble, and Brodir called out, "What's that music?" His voice was high and tense.

Muirtagh grinned. Maelmordha said, "It's Caoilte's song—the music they play when they go riding—the Wild Horsemen." Lower, he said, "Don't play it, Muirtagh, it chills me."

"Oh? Is this better?" He played Dierdre's song, just before her death. Each of the notes hung on the string, quivering, full of a sick high wailing.

"No," the redheaded Dane shouted. "Play something we can smile at."

"Go find your mother. She'll kiss your tears away."

The man leapt up, and Muirtagh snatched for his bow. Two others yanked the Dane back to the bench. Bjorn was on his feet.

"Let him play, you puppies—if you quiver at a song what will you do when the Irish come? I'll kill you all if you stop him." He jerked his head around to face Muirtagh. "Play that wild song, I like that."

Muirtagh grinned at him, at the dark blazing face. "Yes, you would, but I don't, and I'm hungry."

"Play just a little more."

"All right, then." He nodded.

Bjorn sat down, and Muirtagh played them the song of the son of the King of Moy, who met a girl in the greenwood. The whole song was full of sunlight, and he played it twice.

"Play them the ó Cullinane war song," Maelmordha said.

"I've no right to it."

"Play it anyway."

"This harp can't play it. No fault of mine, it's the

harp." He flexed his hands. "Anyway, I'm hungry—did I know I'd starve to death for it, I'd never learned to play so well."

Bjorn reached out and pushed the man beside him off the bench. "Sit down here, harper. And leave that other instrument against the wall."

Muirtagh glanced at the fallen man, who was getting to his feet, and sat down next to Bjorn.

"There was no need for the trickwork," Bjorn said.

"A careful man hedges everything."

Bjorn smiled the child's smile. "A hero cuts down all hedges. Isn't that so?"

"Oh, of course. But if I saw such a chasm open up before me, I'd scream and run."

"You didn't once."

"Don't speak to me of it."

"Why not? It was a great thing to do."

Muirtagh shrugged and cut himself some meat.

"You were hero enough to put an arrow through that peephole."

"I can do that sleeping."

Brodir, across the way, leaned forward and said, "Bjorn, between here and Denmark there's not a modest man; when you find one, be glad of it. I met your brother once, harper."

"What did you think of him?"

"Next to Bjorn I'd sooner have had him on my side in a battle than anyone else. A little slow in the head, maybe, but he was fighting-wild." Brodir's pale eyes moved to Bjorn. "You would have hated him."

Bjorn shrugged. "They don't call me Wolfbrother because I'm madly fond of men."

Brodir shrugged off his cloak; his black hair was so long he had it tucked into his belt. "This one used a sword like a whip. I remember him taller than I am—isn't that so?"

Muirtagh nodded.

"And he had the long arms to match. That sword whistled when he swung it. We never fought." Brodir smiled. "I've often thought it was a pity that we never fought."

Bjorn said to Muirtagh, "Eat. You said you were hungry." To Brodir he said, "You remember how Einar Hauksson would come into a fight? They say he was the tallest man since Rolf the Ganger. I'd as soon meet a tall man; he has to stoop to get down to my size."

Muirtagh listened to him—they talked more and more Danish, and gradually he lost understanding. It was suddenly odd to be in a room full of men, Danes especially.

He remembered the ship, and waited until Bjorn had stopped talking to Brodir to ask him about it.

"Yesterday?"

"Yesterday very late, just before sunset."

"And north of the Cliffs of Howth? Nobody sailed in today. If they're clever they'll stand out and rig a sea anchor. Nobody could sail against the coast when the tide's running. What was her figurehead?"

"I couldn't see it very clearly."

"How big was she?"

"Oh, big. I don't know much about ships."

Bjorn glanced over at Brodir. "Has anybody sighted *Gull's Bride*?"

Brodir laughed. "No, but it may be."

"*Gull's Bride* is my brother's ship," Bjorn said. "One of them. Oh, well, one can always hope."

Brodir laughed again.

After he'd eaten, Muirtagh played a little more, an undercurrent to their talk. He thought of Aud, Eoghan, his

other children, and was surprised that he was unmoved.
The harp was enough, he thought.

In the bright morning he watched ships sail up the
river, already crowded with moored longships. The
dragonheads drifted slowly through the ranks of hulls
and stopped, and he heard the anchors splashing down.
He felt like a small boy truant from his plowing to see
the warriors march by; it was exciting in that same way.
But he couldn't tell if any of the three newcomers was
the ship he had seen that other day.

Bjorn Wolfbrother came up beside him. "That's my
brother Einar," he said. "Einar Bloodletter. We'll have
some pretty fight-play before this tide's ebbing."

"I'll be going then. I've heard of you and your
brother."

"Oh? You don't want to stay and cheer us on, hoping
one of us will kill the other? They all do, you know.
Whenever Einar and I . . . No, you don't. You should
have been a monk."

"You don't have to fight him." Muirtagh sat down on
a piling.

"Of course I do. They'd all be so terribly disappointed."

A skinboat was coming toward them, waddling over
the little waves. In the stern sat a big, blond man. Muirtagh glanced at Bjorn and saw him shift a little, his shoulders hunching slightly. His face looked almost bored.

The skinboat touched the shore and the men leapt out.
Muirtagh saw that a crowd had gathered, up where the
sandy bank gave way to steep overhang. Einar strode
through the waves, his hair and beard plaited, his nose
peeling from the sun.

"In all the world," Einar said, "there are so many men
—why must the first I see always be you?"

"Don't bother with the duller questions," Bjorn said. "I'd see you come out of the water a bit farther down the beach. This is mine. Wade, brother."

Einar looked around. His eyes rested on Muirtagh, and Muirtagh almost flinched.

"It's odd, the men you bring to side you," Einar said. "This one here, like somebody's old figurehead—"

"Whom are you fighting, me or the harper?" Bjorn pointed down the beach. "I said that you should land somewhere else. You'll dirty my sand."

Metal rasped on metal; Einar had drawn his sword. The crowd murmured fiercely. Bjorn swayed a little, setting himself. Muirtagh felt the thews of his body tighten and coil. He hurled himself off the piling, bounded through the waves to the skinboat, and shoved it out into the current.

"Your boat's floating away, Viking," he said. "Hadn't you ought to catch it?"

The water was lapping around his thighs. Nobody laughed. Bjorn's mouth twitched a little. He was staring at his brother, his huge hands hooked in his belt.

"Hnnnnh," Einar said. He turned and went after the boat; the current was whisking it along the beach. He and his men caught it and dragged it up on the shore a little way from Bjorn.

Bjorn said, amused, "Now, that was quick thinking."

"If you're going to fight, please do it when I'm not around. Blood makes me sick at the stomach."

Bjorn laughed, clapped him on the back, and said, "Let's go up on the wall and sit and drink. There's nothing else to do."

"All right."

They walked through the town, getting a jar of mead on their way. Muirtagh said, "Dublin is ruining my peace of mind."

"It's good for your shooting and your harping, though."

They climbed up onto the wall and walked along it to a place where a tall tree threw some shade over the broad earthworks. Bjorn said, "I'm fairly fond of Dublin. I don't usually like towns. In the Southern Isles we have none, only huts slapped up against the hills."

He took a drink out of the mead jar and handed it to Muirtagh. "There's no one on the islands but old women, anyway. And some men's wives, and the littler children."

"You're on the sea always, are you?"

"Almost always. I almost laughed in Einar's face when you pushed the boat off. That was funny."

Muirtagh pulled off his cloak; it was getting warmer. "I didn't think it so, but I was afraid—here he comes."

Bjorn looked over his shoulder at his brother, coming down the wall. "Well, there's no one here, so this will be pleasant. Good morning, womb-fellow."

Einar grunted and sat down, one knee flexed, in the Danish fashion. He drank some mead and set the jar down with a clatter. "All the way from Iceland I come, just to be thrown off the beach by the likes of you two. Who's he?"

"Muirtagh the Harper. He's a good one, too. And good with a bow."

"Tricky hands? Have you heard the story about Shockbow, in the fight where King Olaf was killed?"

"I have. Muirtagh, have you?"

" 'What broke so loud?' Yes."

"That's a good tale," Einar said. "Ketil Greyface said I should tell you if you ever come back to Norway he's going to make you marry his sister."

Bjorn laughed. "Her? Never. Are you Iceland-based now?"

"Yes, over by Swinefell."

"Do you know Flosi?"

"Everybody in Iceland knows everybody else." Einar took another drink of the mead. "Hnnnh. Why don't you get some good wine or beer?"

"Usquebaugh," Muirtagh said.

"Yes." Einar leaned off the wall and shouted to a servant to bring them usquebaugh. "One thing you Irish can do better than the rest of us—and I'll admit it—is drink."

"If you haven't heard the story of Njal's burning," Bjorn said to Muirtagh, "Thorstein Hallson is here who can tell it better than anyone else. That's a tale—my ears curled when I first heard it."

"It curled Gunnar Lambison's ears the last time he heard it," Einar said. "Did you hear of that—were you there?"

"I? No."

"What happened?" Muirtagh said.

"Oh," Einar said. "Gunnar was one of Flosi's men who was at the burning, and in the Orkney Jarl's house told the story—it was at the Yule feast. But Kari Solmundson was listening outside the window. Kari was old Njal's son-in-law and had been on Njal's side in the feud. Gunner slandered Njal and his sons, and Kari broke in and took off Gunnar's head with one slash of the sword."

"In the middle of the Yule feast?"

"Oh, it was wonderful, I've heard—they had to scrub off the table before they could eat."

"Send somebody after your harp," Bjorn said. "Einar, tell him what the Jarl said."

Muirtagh called up an Irish boy who was passing and told him to go to the fort and bring the harp. Einar said, "The Jarl and Flosi both agreed that Kari was in his rights, because there had been no blood-price paid. Flosi and Njal all through that feud paid each other the same sack of money back and forth for blood-price."

"Flosi was sick of the whole thing before it was rightly begun," Bjorn said. "It was his wife who kept it up."

Muirtagh grinned. "I've heard you Danes are something weakhanded about your women."

"Not I," Bjorn said. "I'm not married."

"You will be, if you ever go back to Donnersfjord," Einar said. He tapped Bjorn on the knee. "Ketil says he wouldn't mind it so much if you'd only got her with child once, but this is the second, now, and they're both girls."

"How can he expect me to marry a woman who can produce only girls?" Bjorn started the bung in the little cask of usquebaugh with the hilt of his dagger. "She's a pleasant thing to talk to, though."

"Talk?" Einar put one hand over his eyes. "Woman-hunter that he is, he talks to them."

"Here comes Thorstein," Bjorn said. "It's pleasant to talk to women, Einar. 'What is your name?' 'Do you mind if I tear your dress?' That sort of thing."

Thorstein Hallson came up the wall and shook hands with Einar. He sank down beside them all.

"You were disappointing this morning," he said to Bjorn. He nodded to Muirtagh. "And it was all your fault."

"He wears his bearsark inside out," Bjorn said.

The boy came with the harp, and Muirtagh played a jig on it.

"Don't," Thorstein said, "ask me to tell the story of Njal's burning. I've told it so often I use the same words all the way through. I thought to call every man in Dublin into some great hall and tell it all at once to get it over with."

"Muirtagh tells old stories," Bjorn said, "and pleasantly leaves the morals off. Let me see that." He reached for the harp.

Thorstein said, "I know—I was there, last night. That wild music had them all leaping to look over their shoulders."

"But not you?" Einar said.

Thorstein laughed. "Not me, not Bjorn, not Brodir."

Einar lifted his head. "Brodir—what's he like?"

Thorstein shrugged. "All unafraid. He's fey—you can see it in his face, and he knows it."

"How does one play prettily?" Bjorn said, jangling the strings of the harp.

"One plays before one's hands are knotted from swordplay." Muirtagh took the harp back. "He's an odd one, Brodir."

"Nothing ever bothers him," Bjorn said. "He's got foresight, very strong; he's troll-wise, I think. Maybe that's why he gave up the White Christ."

Muirtagh jerked his head up. "What?"

"Oh, didn't you know that? He's gone back to the old gods."

"They do say that the Christ cursed him," Einar said.

Muirtagh opened his mouth to say something—he could not conceive of Christ cursing a man. But he changed his mind and played the harp.

Two or three girls were walking by the wall, pretending to fetch turf or water or bread. Thorstein shouted at them. All down the wall, the sentries began to yelp and swear at each other, calling to the girls.

Muirtagh played a love song, speaking the words— "She flung down her ivory comb. She threw back her long pretty hair—" One of the girls had stopped and was talking, her eyes cast down, to Bjorn and Thorstein.

Einar said, "I've got my woman on board the *Gull's Bride*. It takes better foresight than Brodir's to come to a place like this and have your bed warm when you creep into it."

"Hold my feet," Bjorn said.

Einar took hold of Bjorn's ankles, and Bjorn slid off the wall, his hands reaching for the girl. She giggled and backed away, her hands clasped behind her, and upside down Bjorn cajoled her and murmured to her, smiling, cocking his head, moving his hands quietly. The girl giggled and came closer, and Bjorn caught her by the wrists.

"Hold tight, Einar."

He tossed her up, swinging her almost into the branches of the tree, and drew himself quickly upright before she could do more than scream. He sat her down in his lap and put his arms around her.

"He is a heart," Muirtagh said to the voice of the harp, "an acorn from the oakwood."

"You're Irish," the girl said.

"Oh, yes."

"Are you from Leinster? Your accent's different."

"Leinster's hills, near the edge of Meath—we were Meathmen until I was half grown."

"Sing another song."

"Do the Vikings have love songs?" Muirtagh asked Einar.

"Hundreds."

Thorstein reached for the usquebaugh. "There's the song the first man sang the first woman, but I've forgotten it."

"Then why bring it up at all?" Einar said.

"Oh, it's something to think of."

"The Irish songs are prettier," the girl said. She snuggled into Bjorn's arms and he licked her ear.

"There's the song Gar Nine-Finger sang to Edith the Grey-eyed, the night he stole her from her father's castle," Thorstein said.

"And you've forgotten that one too, I suppose," Muirtagh said.

"Well, it couldn't have been very good. Some men have the gift of words, but Gar couldn't put three together and have them do more than fetch wine for him."

"You'll never see a man better in a fight," Bjorn said.

"What a berserker he was," Einar said. "No Christian could have kept him out of the fire, if he'd wanted his feet burnt."

"Most of the time he couldn't tell the difference," Thorstein said. "It was drink that finished Gar—mead-rich they called him. He went out one night to make water and forgot he was on his ship. He tried to walk down the moonpath, thinking it was the white pebble road in Nidaros. They found him the next day, floating face down."

"Then how do they know he thought it was the white pebbles in Nidaros?"

"You're reasoning too closely," Muirtagh said. "If it sounds right he did."

Thorstein chewed on his thumbnail a moment. "Look into Brodir's face when you see him, Einar."

"I've seen him before. Big, and rash, and he doesn't dare lose."

"He never loses," Bjorn said. "I'd as soon go up against giants as fight against Brodir."

Muirtagh frowned a little, and Bjorn laughed. "It's bad luck to fight him. I'm fond of my luck."

Two horsemen were galloping in toward the walls. Muirtagh stood up and looked out to see.

"The Kings are coming," one shouted. "They are all coming."

Muirtagh sat down on his heels. "The High King and Maelsechlainn are somewhere near."

Thorstein leaned off the wall. "Open the gates—let the sentries in."

Muirtagh played the jig on the harp. "Leave off the

dancing music," Einar said. "Play us a war song."

"I am." Muirtagh played the jig faster.

He wondered if Eoghan would bring up the ó Cullinanes to fight, if he would meet them in the battle, and what he would do.

A tall, heavy man with a red face was riding through the town on a brown horse. He came toward them slowly—Muirtagh watched him. The Danes even rode differently than Irish.

"What's the matter?" the big man called to them.

"The Irish are coming in," Thorstein shouted.

The big man heaved his cloak up over one arm. "Well, let them come. For this we rode the waves here." He cantered off.

"The Orkney Jarl," Bjorn said to Einar. "He's fat from high living. They promised him Gormflaith, Maelmordha's sister—but she's not here, you'll notice. She's somewhere gone, now that it's all come to fighting."

Brodir rode by, frowning, and Bjorn called to him: "Brodir!" They waved to each other. To Einar, Bjorn said, "Same promise."

He bent his head and stroked his face against the girl's long silken hair. Muirtagh couldn't guess how he kept the crown on his head; it was always pushed far back.

He played a little, and Einar and Thorstein talked about Iceland. Bjorn's hands looked small—they were finely made, long and slender, but when he took hold of the girl's hand the size of his hands was suddenly obvious.

"No wonder you can't play," Muirtagh said. "Your fingers are too big."

Bjorn took the girl's ear gently between his teeth. "I play other harps than yours." The girl yelped. He'd bitten her.

He stood up suddenly and took the girl by the hand,

to lead her away down the wall. "No," she said and shook her head.

"Don't be afraid," he said. "I'm not going to hurt you."

He smiled over her head at Muirtagh. "Much," he said softly. His eyes were smoky. He was holding the girl so fast she could not break free, and she was afraid to cry out and went with him.

"Women will ruin him," Einar said. "He even looks mine up and down."

"She's a nice piece of female flesh," Thorstein said.

"Oh, she passes for a woman, on a foggy night."

Muirtagh got up. "I'm hungry." The smoky look in Bjorn's eyes stayed in his mind and bothered him.

"Wait, I'll come with you," Einar said. "It's hungry work, sitting on walls all day long."

"Are you content?" Maelmordha said.

Muirtagh opened his mouth to answer, scowled, and said, "Now, there's a strange question."

"I thought you'd be all eager to get home."

"I like being here."

"You don't belong here. You look odd here."

"They like my harping."

He played the Cattle Raid of Cooley for them. It was pleasant to have them caught up in it, their hands fists when the music shouted, laughing when the music played some little joke.

In the hall, among all the other men, Bjorn and Einar walked stiff-legged around each other, swaggering, and only Maelmordha's order kept them from fighting. Muirtagh, sitting by the high seat, could see the whole mass of these men, and he saw how the crowd eddied around Bjorn and Einar, how ripples of excitement moved from each of them toward the other. Brodir alone didn't seem to mind it all. He sat quietly on the bench, one hand around his drinking horn, the silver fur around his shoulders.

Slowly, the pack of Danes and Leinstermen settled and calmed. A door opened, and the Orkney Jarl came in, calling out to Brodir in his booming voice. Close behind him walked Sygtrygg. Muirtagh had seen him only once before. He was young, and he swaggered too much. He sat down beside Malemordha.

"I hear the Irish are coming."

Maelmordha nodded. "I sent one of the scouts to you to tell you."

"I sent him away—I was sleepy."

Maelmordha gave him a sour look. "So are you always."

Sygtrygg laughed. "Don't abuse me, dear man. Am I not the reason you've so many fine Vikings to save your rebellion for you?"

The Orkney Jarl, just below them, turned his head. "Be quiet, child. Thorstein. Something's bothering you."

Thorstein scratched his head, plucked out a louse, and stared at it. "What's to be done about the Irish?" He cracked the louse between his nails.

Einar grinned. "You just showed us. Crack them."

"This is a great fat louse," the Orkney Jarl said, "and we must have all our men here."

"They are here, all but a few nithings," Bjorn said.

"Ospak isn't here," Sygtrygg said.

Brodir looked up; Ospak was his brother. "Do you hear nothing, then? Ospak will not come. When I left Man he was careening each of his ten ships by turn, and he'd only got to the third."

Bjorn laughed.

Einar said softly, "Some say it was Ospak who took

the news of our coming to the High King."

Bjorn jerked his head up and glared. Brodir put one hand on his shoulder to hold him down. "Perhaps—Ospak's still a Christian and that goes oddly with some people."

"Not with Ospak," Bjorn said, staring at Einar.

Brodir snorted. "Don't use my brother as an excuse for your fighting. You've never liked Ospak until now."

Einar went off early from the hall, to stand guard— the Orkney Jarl's doing. Bjorn got very drunk. He was in a pleasant mood and told jokes, so that the table rocked with laughter, and in the middle of it all Bjorn sat smiling under his crown and took the casual insults flung at him, shooting back something equal to it.

Muirtagh played again, a trick song of a dialogue between a cat, a dog and a mouse. The harp meowed like a cat, barked like the dog, and squeaked like the mouse, and finally, when the three had decided to live peacefully together, the harp howled like the wolf that came in and ate them all up. The Danes loved it.

"Bjorn is unfond of morals," Muirtagh said. "Or I could point one out to you from that. So much for it. You do some of the work and figure it out yourselves."

Thorstein suddenly brightened, remembering. "Bjorn, what did you do with that girl you had this afternoon?"

Bjorn exaggerated shock. "Spare these tender ears, Thorstein."

"Look here," Sygtrygg said. "I won't have you abusing my people."

"Look here," Bjorn said. "When you called us all in you called all of us in. Am I to be half a man for the niceness of you?"

"Speak civilly to your betters," Sygtrygg said.

"The words out of my mouth."

Maelmordha jerked Sygtrygg back into his seat. "Bjorn, tell me for once what the crown is for?"

Bjorn shrugged. "To hide the balding place."

Muirtagh leaned forward to pour himself usquebaugh; he was sitting between Maelmordha's feet and Syg- trygg's. "I heard a song once of a man who wore a crown, so that someone would knock it off his head and he could kill him for it."

"Sing it," Bjorn said.

"It's bad luck to be sung of, remember?" Muirtagh grinned.

"Why did you mention it, then?"

"When a King asks a question someone must answer it, and I could see you were too bashful."

"How pleasant it must be to be a harper and offend everyone with impunity." Bjorn laughed. "And to be a bowman so that you can be as bad a harper as you want."

"Who wants to be a bad harper?"

"I'm fuddled; it came out wrong. Play something."

After that, when they were all lying down to sleep, Bjorn came over to him in the dark and said, "When this is all done, will you come with me?"

"I'll not settle for less than a crown. You shouldn't plan so far ahead."

"Oh, it's the only way. Out-trick the gods. I mean God."

"Do you need a harper?"

"I want a harper. I need a man who can shoot arrows through peepholes and shove skinboats into the current."

"Pfft."

"I just asked."

"I will. If there's enough of me left to walk on board."

"Good."

Bjorn's breath stank of wine. He went off, bumped

into something, and fell with a crash. In the dark someone swore, something hit something else, and everyone
started fighting. Muirtagh lay still, listening and laughing
until they quieted down and went to sleep.

Muirtagh hauled up the bucket and set it on the edge of the well. Bjorn plunged his whole head in and lifted it out, snorting and swearing. The water dripped down over his ears and turned the shoulders of his shirt dark blue. He wiped the water out of his eyes on his sleeve, clapped on his silver-gilt crown, and stretched.

"Ayyyy-yaah. That makes a difference."

"Push your hair out of your eyes," Muirtagh said. He tossed the bucket back and reeled it up. Scooping up some water with his hand, he sucked it into his mouth and held it there a moment to get rid of the fuzzy taste. Bjorn caught him by the nape of the neck and ducked him, and Muirtagh, lurching back, flung the bucket at Bjorn so that he was drenched.

"Now look what you've done," Bjorn said. He held his soaked shirt away from his body. "It's cold. Ouch."

"You're the one who tried to drown me."

"Watch out or I'll push you in the well."

He laughed, pulling his shirt over his head. Brodir rode through the marketplace and shouted, "Bjorn, have you been new christened?"

Bjorn was waving his wet shirt in the air to dry it. His chest, covered with curly black hair, looked bigger than when he was dressed.

"The harper's a persuasive kind of priest, Brodir," he called.

"Has he offered you Michael for your guardian angel?"

Bjorn flapped the shirt to dry it. "I'm bargaining for Jesus Christ."

There was muttered laughter. Muirtagh, leaning against the well side, said, "A false priest, I." He saw Einar beyond the edge of the crowd. "Here comes your brother, Bjorn."

Bjorn stepped back, his arms drooping, so that his shirt trailed in the dust. His crown had slipped back on his head. "Why, so it is."

Einar had three of his men with him; Bjorn cast around in the crowd until he had collected two of his own, who stood behind him, their faces expressionless. Einar moved heavily forward, until he was only a few steps from the well, and the other people pushed back so that he and his men stood alone.

"I'm going to drink that water," Einar said, and pointed to the well.

Bjorn looked around him, saw the full bucket on the edge of the well, and tipped it so the water spilled out into the street. "Drink it, brother mine."

He tossed his shirt to Muirtagh. Einar advanced a little, set his hands on his belt, and said, "Isn't it cold, wee thing? Too cold to be going about without your clothes on."

"The weather never hurt a good Viking," Bjorn said. "Go on, drink."

He spat into the well. Einar howled wordlessly, backed up a few steps, and came rushing forward, his men left behind. Bjorn dodged out of his way, circling him, his huge hands loose. Einar pulled up alongside the well, a little way from Muirtagh.

They began to circle, calling each other names and swearing. The marketplace was packed, and Brodir, on his big bay horse, looked nervous. He crowded his horse into the center of the watchers.

"God," Bjorn said. "All back and no head. Come on, Einar, fight me."

"Stand still, you little—"

They lunged forward, grappling, their hands clawing

over each other's shoulders, and for an instant hung together, braced and balanced. Einar lost his grip on Bjorn's naked shoulders and Bjorn's left leg whipped around and tripped him. Einar fell heavily. Bjorn picked up his crown from where it had fallen and tossed it to Muirtagh.

"Hold that for me."

Einar was on his feet again, and prowling. They circled, wary. Muirtagh brushed the dust off the edge of the crown.

"Pig's trick," Einar was saying. "Pig's trick, you pig."

"Any boy ought to learn—hah!"

They leapt together. Bjorn jumped, missed his hold, and Einar caught him by the wrist. He snapped him like a whip and Bjorn flew into the crowd. He came up roaring and dove straight for Einar. They went down, rolled around a little, and leapt up and apart, coated with dust and panting.

Bjorn's hand fell to his belt, where his dagger was. Brodir spurred his horse in between them.

"Enough of that," he said. "Put it up, Bjorn."

Bjorn snorted through his nose, clapped the dagger down into the sheath, and strutted over to the well. He put his shirt on and set his crown carefully on his head. Einar stood by watching, disheveled.

"Come on," Bjorn said. "This place stinks."

He and his men and Muirtagh went off. As soon as they were out of the marketplace, Bjorn said, "I can't do that properly, that jump trick."

"What are you supposed to do?"

"Get him around the waist, drop him, and start squeezing." Bjorn spat out muddy saliva. "Do you wrestle?"

"No."

"It's a Northerner's game. You ride horses, we wrestle. That's why I have short legs and you have long legs."

"Are you full brothers, you and Einar?"

"I trust my mother—yes. Why?"

"Oh, you're so different. My brother was big and blond, too."

Bjorn shrugged. "He's thick in the head."

Brodir went to a witch that day, and came back with a prophecy that made no one feel any better. If they fought before Good Friday, King Brian would win out, but if they fought on Good Friday, the Irish would win and King Brian would die. Brodir rode back and forth along the wall, brooding.

The Orkney Jarl said something about never wanting to be King of Ireland anyway. Sygtrygg was staying in his room, alone, and they said he was gnawing his fingernails down to the quick. A few more ships anchored in the river; Bjorn said that a man could walk from bank to bank across the ships without wetting his feet.

Thorstein and Einar bet him that he couldn't. They all went off to the river so that Bjorn could prove what he'd said. Muirtagh, Thorstein and one of Brodir's men named Erling took a skinboat out to watch, in case Bjorn should cheat by swimming once he was among the ships. They rowed out a little way, and Bjorn started off from the beach.

The first step was easy enough; two of the Orkney longships were drawn up on the shore, where it was level. Bjorn walked out to the stern of one, waited until the current swung the next ship's bow toward him, and jumped. He hit the dragon's head, slid along it, and tumbled over into the hull. Erling, who was rowing, swung the skinboat around that ship.

Bjorn was standing on the gunwale, staring at the next ship, a good distance away. It was anchored fore and aft. He thought a while and got down from the gunwale.

A few moments later they saw an oar thrusting out

through the lock amidships. Bjorn lashed it with rope from the ship and started out along the oar.

"Let's go knock him off," Thorstein said.

"Foul," Muirtagh said.

"Oh, but can't you see the look on his face?"

"Look at the one he's wearing now," Erling said.

Bjorn was part way out on the oar, balancing, just where his weight began to bend it. He was wobbling, and his face was agonized. He took a deep breath, flailed wildly with his arms, and almost fell sideways off the oar. Suddenly he regained his balance. He ran lightly out along the sagging oar, and just at the point where he could not have kept his footing, he leapt for the other ship.

"Miss," Thorstein shouted. Bjorn landed hard across the gunwale, and obviously the shock had knocked the wind out of him. He was sliding toward the water. A swan sailed by, looked up curiously, and stopped to watch. Bjorn hauled himself up into the ship.

Muirtagh glanced toward the Dublin shore and saw a yelling mob there. He looked back just in time to see Bjorn leap into the next ship, the last before the far bank, and an easy jump from the previous ship. Now he had only the bank to reach.

"Look," Erling said softly, and nodded to the far shore.

Muirtagh craned his neck. Three horsemen were reined up, a little way down the river, and close to the bank. They were Irish.

"He hasn't got a sword," Thorstein said.

"None of us has. Bjorn—"

Bjorn waved at him.

"Bjorn, give it up."

Bjorn waved again, impatiently, and walked aft.

"Pull for the shore," Muirtagh said. "He's raising the

stern anchor, he'll let it drift in."

"That's not fair," Thorstein said. "The wager's off."

"Pull."

Erling rowed hard; Bjorn had an oar out and was poling the ship in toward the bank. Muirtagh wasn't sure he'd seen the Irish.

The longship's stern hit the bottom, and Bjorn leapt, the oar in both hands over his head, onto the bank. He gave the longship a shove that thrust it back out into the river and ran toward the skinboat. The Irish galloped after him.

Halfway to the skinboat, with a horse almost on him, Bjorn whirled and swung the oar. The oar was cumbersome, hard to whip around, but when it hit the oncoming horse it took the legs out from under him. Bjorn leapt for the rider. The other two horses had been headed for the skinboat. Now they swerved and charged Bjorn. One of the Irish had a lance; he lifted it. Bjorn straightened above the fallen Irishman, reared back, and threw something. One horse fell heavily into the grass, and the lance bounced off the ground near Bjorn. He ran for it, but the other Irishman was veering away, riding off. Bjorn raced for the skinboat, leaving the lance behind.

He climbed in—the boat barely floated. Erling rowed carefully. The water lapped at the very edge of the boat's rim, and they were all sitting on each other.

The swan was coming back, staring at them. They got out into the current, and the water began to pour in.

"Out," Bjorn cried, and dove overboard. Thorstein and Erling followed him without hesitation. Muirtagh, left in sole possession of a boat he couldn't row, sat still, waiting for the wild rocking to subside. The boat was riding much higher, and it settled almost at once. Muirtagh felt perfectly safe and just as helpless.

"How do I make this thing move?" he shouted.

"Row it."

Bjorn swam up. "Oars," he said. "Just row it."

"I don't know how." Muirtagh picked up the oars and put them awkwardly into the water. The boat began to spin around in place.

"No, no," Bjorn cried. "Like this." Treading water, he made motions with his hands.

Muirtagh shrugged and tried. One blade of the oar hit the water on its flat, and spray showered over Bjorn.

"Push me," Muirtagh said. He pulled the oars in.

Bjorn sputtered. Thorstein and Erling swam over and they conferred. The swan steered for them; coming up behind Erling, it pecked him in the head. Erling howled and they beat off the swan.

"Hurry," Muirtagh said. "We'll be in the ships in a minute."

They swam together to the stern of the little boat and began to push. Erling rubbed his head and glanced over at the swan, which was watching them with a vicious eye; Erling swore.

Muirtagh sat in the stern, his arms crossed, and grinned at them. When they were almost to the Dublin bank, Bjorn cried, "Now," and threw all his weight on the boat's stern.

The boat tipped over. Muirtagh plunged into the cold water. Looking up, he saw the sunlight coming in through the green water, wrinkled and murky. He had a sudden vision of being drowned, weed in his hair, puffy-faced. His foot touched bottom and he thrust himself up above the surface.

The others were laughing at him. "I can't swim," he called, and with a gasp went under again. The water bound his arms.

Hands caught his shoulders and jerked him up. Somebody was hanging onto his chin to keep it above water.

He started to catch at them, frightened they'd let him go again, but one of them grabbed his wrist. "Lie still," Bjorn's voice said. "Lie still."

He lay still in the water, shivering, and they towed him in to shore. Einar was waiting, standing spraddle-legged.

"Well," he said, "you got wet enough."

"I crossed dry."

"But it wasn't fair to up anchor on that ship," Thorstein said. "We won the wager—you'd never have gotten to the other side without that."

"There was nothing in the wager about moving the ships. Only getting across dry."

"It wasn't fair. Muirtagh, what do you say?"

"He's right. There was nothing in the wager about moving ships."

Bjorn had his crown back on; he was squeezing out the water in his shirt tails. "I won."

"Ask Thorgeist. He's a lawyer." Einar went off to find Thorgeist.

"Besides," Bjorn said, "I did a little fighting in between trips. That should count for something."

Thorgeist settled the dispute in Bjorn's favor. Einar stood talking to a tall woman with a long rope of blond hair over one shoulder. She laid one hand on Einar's arm, smiled at Bjorn, and walked off along the shore.

"That's my brother's lovely wife," Bjorn said softly.

"Are Danish women all beautiful?"

"Only Vikings' wives." Bjorn was staring after her.

"What's her name?"

"Aud."

Muirtagh choked. Bjorn looked at him. "Are you sick? Did you swallow any water?"

"No," Muirtagh said. His Aud's clear grey eyes hovered in his mind.

Einar came up to Bjorn and said, "Don't you look at my woman that way." He shoved him.

Bjorn knocked Einar's hand down, snarled at him, and stalked off. Muirtagh ran to catch up with him. Bjorn was muttering in the language of the Southern Isles.

"How can I fight him if I take his wife?"

"Don't take his wife."

Bjorn gasped, his eyes shut. "Don't say that."

"She's taller than you are."

"On their backs all women are the same height."

"I've never had but one."

"We'll have to rectify that. What was her name?"

Muirtagh smiled. "Aud."

Bjorn cocked his head. "Oh. Well. At least you wouldn't encounter my worst problem."

"What?"

"Calling them by different names. Odin's my witness. Just at a most tender moment I will call Thyra Hallgerda, and the next thing I know I'm standing in my shirt in the cold." He shook his head.

Aud had whispered his name in his ear, clung to him, argued with him—screamed and wept in childbed for him. "I don't think you know much about women," Muirtagh said.

"I know everything a man can know about women." Bjorn nodded his head emphatically.

Yet, here was another Aud, a Danish Aud.

"Is that a common name in Irish women?" Bjorn said.

"Is Einar's wife Irish?"

"Her mother was from Galloway."

Bjorn started off on the tale of a woman he'd known once. They walked up to the fort to sit and drink and tell stories, and Maelmordha came in and said that Brodir, the Orkney Jarl and he had figured out a way to avoid the witch's prophecy.

"Fight on Easter," Muirtagh said.

Maelmordha shook his head. "No. We haven't got enough food in the city to last much past Good Friday, anyway. Not and feed warriors. The Irish are camped over between here and the cliffs by Howth."

"There were some on the far bank this afternoon," Bjorn said. "They may try to get in and burn the ships."

"I'll see to that. There is a weir—what you Vikings call a hop—just beyond the Kings' camp. Brodir's going to take his ships out of the river tonight, sail around to the weir, and anchor there. We'll all go out before dawn tomorrow, and they'll be surrounded—caught between Brodir and us. Brodir's taking all his men and half of Orkney's."

"When is the tide high tomorrow?" Bjorn said.

"Just at dawn. He'll be able to get into the weir then."

"Tomorrow's Good Friday."

"Yes. If they don't surrender when they see we're all around them, we'll have to fight, but I think the Kings will get up and leave when they see us all around."

Bjorn shrugged. "What if they attack Brodir when he's just landing?"

"He'll anchor out in the weir and hold them off until we get there."

"It sounds . . . all right."

"Thank you," Maelmordha said quietly, "for your approval."

He got up and left. Thorstein went after him to talk, and Einar, Bjorn and Muirtagh were left alone in the hall.

Muirtagh got out his harp and played part of Dierdre's song. Einar said, "My woman wants you to play for her, sometime."

Bjorn's head jerked a little. Muirtagh said, "I will." He tuned up one string.

"What did you do to that man whose horse you knocked down with the oar?" Einar said.

Bjorn lifted his head; his eyes were smoky. "I killed him."

"It must have been like swinging a pine tree."

They were going to fight. Muirtagh's stomach muscles gathered. It had seemed somehow that the fighting wouldn't come. They'd stay here forever, like this.

"I heard you found a new island," Einar said.

"Oh, yes," Bjorn said. "It's gone now."

"Sunk beneath the sea," Muirtagh said.

Bjorn glanced at him. "It was very stormy. There were no springs on the island, so the rain was good. Lots of reefs. And the whole made of soft pink sand."

Muirtagh played Oisin, thinking of Finnlaith.

"You don't believe me, do you?" Bjorn said to him.

"I don't not believe you."

"There were trees like the ones in Kerry. And the flowers—the place was full of flowers."

Muirtagh grinned. Bjorn sprang up. "Say something. Tell me you don't believe me."

Muirtagh jumped, startled. He stared at Bjorn, at his eyes. He'd forgotten that Bjorn was dangerous, that Bjorn was to be afraid of. Muirtagh set the harp on the table. His palms were suddenly sweaty. "I can only talk when I want to say something."

"Say something now. Talk, harper. You're so good at talking."

Muirtagh glanced at Einar. The blood was hammering in his ears. "Not just for your sake."

Bjorn flung himself toward him and hit Muirtagh across the face. Muirtagh slid across the floor on his back, rolled to his feet, and ran for the door into the sleeping room. Bjorn like a night-walker was on his back. The

great hands fastened on his shoulders. They fell hard together, and Muirtagh writhed out of Bjorn's grasp. He
struggled toward the door. Bjorn hit him in the back and
knocked him down again, and, flipping over, Muirtagh
got both feet on Bjorn's chest and shoved him away.
Lunging to his feet, he bolted through the door and
slammed it. In the semi-dark he groped for his bow on
the far wall.

The door smashed open. Muirtagh whirled, the bow in
his hands unstrung. "Don't come any closer."

"Put that toy down and fight me."

Muirtagh strung the bow and snatched up an arrow.
"Go away. Leave me alone."

Bjorn's hands fisted. "Sleep with that thing beside you,
strung."

He went out again, and the door slammed.

Muirtagh sank down, the bow across his knees. His
harp was out there. He couldn't stay in here, sitting here,
all day, all night, with his bow strung. But if he went
outside . . .

Bjorn, murderer at his christening. Muirtagh got up,
carrying the bow and two arrows in his left hand, and
unlatched the door. Bjorn and Einar were still at the
table, saying nothing, the jug between them. He walked
to where his harp lay on the table, picked it up, and they
said nothing and didn't look at him. He went to the door
and opened it to go outside. Einar turned his face toward him, his eyes blank, looking through him. Muirtagh
unstrung the bow and went out into the streaming sunlight.

He went to the marketplace to get water for his mare,
and met Thorstein. Thorstein said, "Where's your
friend?"

"We fought," Muirtagh said. He hoisted the bucket

and emptied it into his waterskin.

"Oh, well," Thorstein said. "That should pass by dinnertime."

Muirtagh threw the bucket back down the well. "No," he said. "There was nobody else there but Einar."

Thorstein's brows flew together. Muirtagh went off to water the mare.

He hid the harp in her manger, where he could get at it easily. She was beginning to show the foal inside her. She butted him playfully, and he stood beside her brushing the dust and straw from her hide with his hand, while she drank the water and nosed at the hay over the harp. The stable door opened and his head jerked around, but it was only Brodir, leading in his bay horse.

"Oh. The harper. Good afternoon."

"Good afternoon."

Brodir put up his horse and threw his gear into a corner of the long stable. He wandered over to Muirtagh.

"That's a fine mare. Was the stallion as good?"

"The ó Ruairc's prize."

"Oh? As good as Maelmordha's grey?"

"Better."

Brodir put one hand on the mare's rump, and she kicked at him. Muirtagh talked her calm again and said, "She's not so gentle as she might be."

"I heard some talk you and Bjorn had fallen out."

Muirtagh shrugged; the mare butted him and he combed her mane through his fingers, picking out the bits of straw.

"Would you take it ill if I said you are safe in my company?"

"I'm safe enough where I am."

"Bjorn's an odd man."

"Yes."

"If I gave you my protection he'd not try to touch you. He knows better than to run counter to me. I could use a harper."

"I'd . . . rather . . . No. Thank you."

"No matter. Goodbye."

Brodir went off along the wall and out the door. I am a prize to be collected, Muirtagh thought. A thing to mark a great man. He put his face against the mare's soft neck and shut his eyes; suddenly he hated them all.

"Will you play for us, Muirtagh?" Maelmordha said at dinner, his eyes shifting from Bjorn to Muirtagh and back.

Muirtagh laid his knife beside his plate. "That cold weather's frozen my hands, King."

"They say a coward's hands are always cold," Bjorn said softly, looking at his meat.

"Easily warmed up in a bearsark," Muirtagh said.

"Were you referring to me, coward?"

"In the summer, do you wear fur mittens? I said nothing to you."

He looked up and found Bjorn's flat stare on him. All the planes in Bjorn's face were flattened subtly in his anger; the bones of his face seemed like iron under the taut skin.

"I say you are a coward," Bjorn said, overloud.

Muirtagh stared at him a moment and nodded. "Yes. You've said so three times; such things grow stale when they're repeated. Here, sit down, you keep us all from eating."

He went back to cutting his meat. The sound of his knife was brittle in the silence. Finally, Brodir said, "Sit, Bjorn. He doesn't mean to fight you."

The bench scraped, and the small noises of eating

began again. Muirtagh glanced at Bjorn and saw him bent over his plate, his eyes downcast, and his ears red, like a young boy's.

The dinner was short, because Muirtagh would not play, because Brodir wanted sleep before he left. Muirtagh sat in the hall, in a corner, and listened to the general talk. Whenever he thought of fighting his stomach writhed.

Maelmordha said, "What did you fight over?"

Muirtagh jumped. "You startled me."

"I'm sorry." Maelmordha sat down. "I told you not to stay here."

"Oh, well."

Across the hall someone laughed, stark in the low murmur.

"Are you afraid?" Maelmordha said. "Of tomorrow."

"Yes," Muirtagh said.

"You weren't afraid of Bjorn. We all saw that."

Hot anger leapt into Muirtagh's throat. "Afraid of Bjorn? He's an honorable man—he's vulnerable that way, to one like me."

"I shouldn't have brought you into this."

"You never brought me into it."

"Nevertheless, I'm sorry."

"King, you are always sorry."

Muirtagh got up and walked away from Maelmordha. What he had said to Bjorn made him recoil from himself. He went into the sleeping room—at the door he stopped and turned, and, looking out, saw Bjorn in the midst of them all, separate from them all, staring at nothing and smiling. At nothing. Muirtagh shut the door softly behind him.

Tomorrow would settle it. Tomorrow would prove everything. Prove Bjorn right, perhaps, or prove them both wrong. This time it would be only what was to be done, no turning it aside and no turning aside himself. No high words, only killing.

Einar was sitting on a bench, pulling off his shoes and groaning. Muirtagh sank down on the next bench and unlaced his leggings.

"He knows you are no coward," Einar said.

"I know."

"He won't hurt you. He likes you too much. He just wants—"

"I know what he wants. Let him tear me to pieces and take only that he wants."

He rolled himself up in the robes and lay down. His body was whipped tired. Lying still, he listened to the other men come into the room, murmuring to one another and making the benches creak, and he turned his face to the wall and shut his eyes. Tomorrow would settle it all.

"Everybody awake in here. Up, all of you. Wake up."
Muirtagh leapt to his feet, startled. The other men
in the dark room were rushing about, and he heard
the clatter of mail shirts. He groped for his bow and arrowcase, scooped up his shoes, and trotted out into the
hall; Maelmordha was there, being buckled into his
leather coat.

"Brodir's almost there by now," he said. "We have to
go out and support him."

Men streamed into the hall. "How will we cross the
river?" Muirtagh said. He sat down to put on his shoes.

"Bjorn showed us how—we've made a bridge out of
the ships."

Einar had jumped onto the table and was bellowing.
His men fought their way through the mob to him, and
he stepped down. The door out into the yard slammed
open. Through it the violet dawn light flooded into the
room.

"Stay by me," Maelmordha said. "Let's go."

They went out to the stable and got their horses. The
town below the fort was packed with men, all now gathered up around their captains, shoving toward the bridge
of boats. Maelmordha rode up to the head of the crowd,
where the Orkney Jarl was, and said, "Is Sygtrygg coming?"

The Jarl shook his head. "You deserved a better
nephew, Maelmordha."

"Oh, well."

The dragon's heads and tails had been taken down
from the ships, and planks laid from gunwale to gunwale.
The chestnut mare fought madly against crossing, but
the sheer press of the army behind carried her onto the
bridge and she galloped across. Maelmordha's big grey

raced beside her. The Leinstermen ran along after Maelmordha, carrying their spears over their shoulders. Behind them, the Danes trotted, axes and swords in their
belts, and their great shields slung over their backs.

The dawn was slow in coming. Clouds filled the sky;
only in the east was it clear, and there sullen light was
thrusting over the bay. Maelmordha's face was indistinct,
even so close to Muirtagh. They started off toward the
cliffs of Howth. The eagerness of the men behind them
made the horses dance and strike out with their fore
hoofs.

"It's cold," Maelmordha said, frowning.

"It will warm up soon enough," the Orkney Jarl answered. "One way or another."

He turned to look at Muirtagh. "Did you bring your
harp?"

Muirtagh made his stiff lips smile. "No. Shall I have
need of it, Lord?"

The Jarl laughed and settled back, looking straight
ahead.

When they were halfway to the weir—the sun had
finally risen—a rider loped up toward them out of the
wood there. Maelmordha reined in and shouted to him to
name himself.

"Olaf Ormsson, from Brodir's company—they've am-
bushed us. They are burning the ships."

The Danes behind them roared. Maelmordha put his
horse into a lope. The chestnut mare's leap forward almost threw Muirtagh. Behind, weapons clanked and feet
pounded. Muirtagh clung to the mare, keeping her from
outrunning Maelmordha's grey, and tried not to think.

They charged over the plain, through the straggling
edge of the wood, and were among the ships before they
could take it all in. The Irish and Brodir's men were
fighting on the shore of the inlet, screaming and howling.

a tangle of arms and flying hair. Two ships were burnt to the waterline but the others had been anchored safe in the middle of the weir.

A horn blew somewhere. The Irish wheeled to face the oncoming Danes and Leinstermen. The wild charge carried Muirtagh and Maelmordha together into the mass of faces and bodies ahead of them. Maelmordha roared something. His sword was out. Muirtagh clutched mane and reins. Irish voices shrieked in his ears, and his legs scraped shoulders, heads. He thought he was falling and clamped his knees tight to the mare's sides. Lances and swords thrust at him. Abruptly they were beyond the thick of it, and stopping, and when he looked back he saw that the Irish were racing away up to the rise to the west.

"It didn't work," Maelmordha said.

The Orkney Jarl trotted up, his face flushed. "We'll have a new day for it, at least. Brodir?"

Brodir strode through the army. The captains were gathering up their men and making them rest.

"Do we fight?" Maelmordha said, low.

Brodir nodded. "They won't leave us alone, now. They knew we were coming in—they hid in the trees there." He waved his arm at the wood.

The cold dawn made Muirtagh shiver. His bow was still sheathed under his knee. He looked out at the Irish. They had formed up in a long line across the middle of the slope, between two arms of the wood. Behind them, hard against the wood, were some tents, fires—a camp. Before one tent a man stood, and the wind stirred a long white beard.

"There's the King," Muirtagh said.

"Where's Maelsechlainn?" Brodir said. "Maelmordha, send someone to find him—he's not here."

eined off a little. The King would not fight,

old man that he was, but messengers were trotting down from his tent to the Irish lines and back again. The Irish lines rippled and swayed, as if the wind blew them.

Brodir shouted. His men surged up and raced down to make a solid block of bodies, to the right of where Maelmordha stood beside his grey horse. Bjorn would be there, leaning on his shield, with Einar beside him, and his dark face smiling, perhaps. Now the Jarl was riding down to the space between his men and Brodir's, and, calling out, he brought his army down even with Brodir's, to Brodir's left.

"Come along, Muirtagh."

He and Maelmordha rode to the far left of the line, where the Leinstermen were walking back and forth, craning their necks. Maelmordha rode among them, talking quietly to this one and that, Muirtagh trailing him like a trained dog.

A mounted man jogged up and said that Maelsechlainn was off behind the wood, and by the look of his camp he meant to have breakfast and a quiet day before him.

"You were right," Maelmordha said.

He turned to shout at some archers, who turned obediently and walked to the left of the whole of the line, almost against the trees. Muirtagh started off to join them but Maelmordha caught him by the sleeve. "Stay here. They can't shoot, and you'll be more help to me where I can tell you what to shoot at."

Muirtagh's face grew hot. He strung his bow and took the top off the arrowcase. Maelmordha knew he was frightened.

"Maelmordha," Brodir shouted—his voice seemed to come from half the world away.

A horseman was riding out from the High King's army. Maelmordha said, "I'll have to go talk to him, I guess."

"Yes," Muirtagh said. "Give him my . . . greeting. That's Eoghan."

Maelmordha started and peered at the oncoming rider. "So it is."

He walked the grey horse forward, his sword still in its sheath. Eoghan had dismounted and was standing quietly beside his horse, his reins in his hands, midway between the two armies. He seemed taller, broader in the shoulders, his long hair yellow in the early light. Brodir, the Jarl and Maelmordha all were going to meet him.

Muirtagh wanted them all to know that he was Eoghan, that he was Muirtagh's son. The boy stood so quietly there. The three great men faced him and even from here Muirtagh could see that Eoghan looked them each in the face; he took a deep breath and held it a moment, watching.

Maelmordha and the Jarl were galloping back, and the tall boy on the black pony rode at a jog off to the Irish lines. Brodir on foot sauntered toward his men. It was full day. Maelmordha swung around beside Muirtagh, took his sword from its sheath, and raised it. He glanced down at Muirtagh and said, "A well-brought-up boy, that," and he swept the sword down through the air.

They started forward, trotting across the plain, and the Irish lines rolled down to meet them. Their voices rose, a murmur, a grumble, at last a great thunder, and they crashed together. Muirtagh took two steps forward, drawn irresistibly, and Maelmordha caught him by the shoulder and held him back. The two lines wavered and surged up again. Half the Irish gave way in a sudden rush, and the Danes—Brodir's men—screamed and chased them. The axes and swords rose and drew the hot blood after them.

"There," Maelmordha said, touching Muirtagh's shoulder.

Muirtagh set an arrow to the bow, raised it, and drew the string to his ear. He lifted the bow another two fingers and shot. The arrow hurtled up over the edge of the fighting men and dove into the breast of one of the two men fighting Einar. Einar whirled and killed the other. Muirtagh shot another arrow, trying to kill a man in bright gold in the middle of the Irish, but he missed.

"Who were you shooting for?" Maelmordha said.

"The King's son, there." Muirtagh nocked another arrow.

"Ah," Maelmordha said. "The chessplayer."

Muirtagh lifted the bow and shot. Deep inside the tangle of men, the man in the gold whirled, catching at his arm, and looked up. The Irish around him bundled him back to the safety of the camp, and Maelmordha laughed.

"He'll be back," Muirtagh said.

Two Danes broke out of the surging mass and raced up the slope, one clutching at his side. A little band of Irish chased them, and Muirtagh drove them back with arrows.

The other archers were doing nothing, and Maelmordha sent a runner over to tell them to keep the Irish from chasing wounded Danes into the camp. One of the Danes got another sword and ran right back, but the wounded one sat and let two women bandage him up. He lashed a shield tight over his wounded side, picked up his axe, and plunged down the plain again into the battle.

"Get that messenger," Maelmordha said.

A horseman was galloping from the King's tent. Muirtagh shot once and missed; he put an arrow between his teeth, nocked another, and shot. The horse fell hard. The messenger, thrown over the horse's head, lay a moment, got up, and trotted forward. Muirtagh put an arrow through his head.

"Quickly. There."

Six more Danes were rushing up the slope, widely separated. The Irish in a small tide yelped after them. Muirtagh shot as fast as he could put the arrows to the string. The Irish lagged and finally darted back into the fighting. The six Danes, panting, jogged into the camp, tended wounds, got more weapons, ate. They talked, their voices only a little tighter than usual, and ran back.

"Here they come," Maelmordha said. "I knew they'd think of it."

Muirtagh knelt to steady himself. Eight or ten Irish on horses were galloping over around the end of the battle, headed for the edge of the wood. The Irish line could hold that wood against the Danes, and it would cover these horsemen close enough that they could get near Maelmordha. Muirtagh shot at the horses, the big targets, and downed three, but the riders jumped up and, crouching, ran into the shelter of the wood. Muirtagh shot two men before they were all safe among the trees.

Maelmordha fetched a tall shield and moved his horse around so that he could hold the shield over Muirtagh. From the wood came arrows, pelting gently into the grass some way away. Muirtagh shrugged. The range was too long. Wait.

"Fetch us some wine here," Maelmordha shouted.

A woman's shadow stretched across the ground before them. Muirtagh saw the shadow's hands lift a cup toward Maelmordha, and when the cup came to him he took it and drank. He shot carefully into the ragged lines, keeping one eye on the wood.

Before them the plain was mud, churned up by the slow stepping of the warriors' feet, the new grass bruised and broken down. The noise was muffled and strange. A shriek would pierce it, or a sudden crash of sword on sword. The Irish were pushing steadily forward against

Brodir's men, but the Jarl and his men were hammering
in through the center. Once there was a great shout,
sharper than steel, and everybody rushed to one point
and drew as quickly back, leaving something red and
ugly on the ground.

"Watch," Maelmordha snapped.

The Irish hidden in the wood were creeping out toward them. Crouched in the high grass, they appeared
and disappeared. Muirtagh murmured, "Move."

Maelmordha's leg, close by his ear, moved sharply, and
the horse stepped quickly back. Muirtagh shot the arrow
he had nocked, snatched up his case, and darted back toward the weir's shore. He knelt on the lower ground.

He had killed one. The others leapt up and raced for
Maelmordha; still bent over, now they were black
against the skyline for Muirtagh. He shot quickly and
without pausing to watch, aiming for the men in the
front of the charge. Three reared up and slid down into
the grass and the others flattened themselves on the
ground. Maelmordha was shouting.

He whirled his horse and charged the Irish. An arrow
bounced off his shield. He paused, and his sword stabbed
straight down. Two Irish sprang for him. Muirtagh shot
one—he saw the arrow cut an arc against the sky when
the man fell. The other Maelmordha killed. Muirtagh ran
back.

"That was them all," Maelmordha said.

Muirtagh jerked the arrow out of the back of a dead
man. "They should have trusted their bows."

"Oh," Maelmordha said with a laugh. "They wanted
to kill me with their bare hands, I expect."

A roar almost drowned him out. They jerked around
toward the battle—the Leinstermen were rushing up
after a retreating mass of Irish. Muirtagh scurried around,
recovering arrows and watching. The Irish suddenly

held their ground, and the Leinstermen fell back, and now it was the Irish who crowded forward, screaming.

Maelmordha galloped down a little and called out, his voice high and driving. The Jarl sent some of his own men into the advancing Irish, and they flinched away. Maelmordha's voice whipped his men back to fill up the gaps and the lines swayed and steadied.

Two Irish had broken through the rear of the Danish line and were running wildly toward the end of the battle to get back to their friends. Caught up in their own fighting, none of the Danes chased them. They were nearly to the wood; Muirtagh shot at them, but it was too far.

Out of the battle Bjorn ran, bent over, his bearsark wrapped for a shield around his left arm. Like a pacing wolf he ran down the two Irish. He leapt on the first, who never turned his face toward him, but died with his head thrown back. Bjorn sprang without a pause to the other, who had wheeled. Their swords rang out, clashing. Bjorn thrust the Irishman's sword aside and drew his arm back and stabbed, and the Irishman shrieked and fell. Bjorn whirled and darted back into the battle.

The Jarl was jogging up the hill, his face bright red and running sweat. He had a cut across the cheekbone. To Maelmordha he called, "I'm too old and fat for this." He drank from a jug of mead and tossed it down, empty. Swinging, he summoned up two boys for runners and sent them down to tell his men to draw their line out more.

Muirtagh stood beside Maelmordha, watching. Maelmordha said, "Don't forget to shoot."

"Oh."

"Wait. Don't. They're calling a truce."

The Irish all down the line were drawing back, leaving a wide space between the two armies, and Brodir was waving at Maelmordha. Maelmordha lifted his arm and nodded. Everybody set about gathering up the dead and wounded and carrying them back to their camps.

Muirtagh looked into the Irish camp. The King was out of his tent, watching it all. He took some of his men aside and talked to them, pointing this way and that. Finally, he pointed straight up to Maelmordha and said something, nodding his head several times.

One of the men he spoke to stepped forward and shook his head. He and the King seemed to argue, and at last the man shrugged and jogged off, taking his friends with him. When some dozen or sixteen were together, they all started off on a circle that would take them to the wood on the far right.

Muirtagh unstrung his bow and went over to the wine casks. He found a stray cup. Bjorn was coming up the shore toward him, from one of the burnt ships. Muirtagh dipped the cup into the wine and drank; the wine ran cold over the rim and down his chin.

"This killing is dry work," Bjorn said. He scooped up some wine with his hand.

"So," Muirtagh said.

"You almost hit that one I was chasing. It was the longest shot I've ever seen."

"I miss more than I hit."

"I saw you hit one clear across the battle."

"From where I am it's closer to the Irish camp than to the far end of the line."

"What's happening down at that end?"

"They're sending men into the wood."

"Oh. Nothing serious, of course."

He flung back his head and smiled. "Come down and see us, if you find it dull up here. It's something leisurely —we push, they push back."

A horn sounded, whimpering, and Bjorn swung

around. "Oh, the gods. I mean God. Here we go at it again."

He ran off, shouting, waving his men toward him. Muirtagh walked over to where Maelmordha, Brodir and the Jarl had their heads together. Brodir was digging up the turf with the tip of his axe. The horn had been Irish; all the Irish were drawn up on the same line they'd come to that morning, looking grim. The field between them and the Danes was torn up, plowed like a new garden, riven and stained with blood. Overhead of them all the kites and crows swept on their wide wings.

"They are filling that wood with men," the Jarl said. "Brodir, can we take any men out of your part of the line?"

"They are swamping me," Brodir said. "We're one to their two. Send the archers." He looked up at Muirtagh. "Send the harper, these others hit only their own hands."

"Muirtagh," Maelmordha said, "can you go into that wood and clear them out?"

"Alone?"

Maelmordha grinned. "We'll send those others with you, I imagine."

"They'd kill him before he ever got there," the Jarl said.

"Put him on a horse," Brodir said, digging at the turf. "And Bjorn. Let them ride straight to the end of the battle. Bjorn can leave him there, and he'll get to the trees quickly enough."

"Bjorn would have his head off before they'd gone two strides," the Jarl said.

"No," Muirtagh said. "But please stop talking as if only I were going."

Brodir turned and shouted for Bjorn. One of Maelmordha's men led up the chestnut mare; the Jarl was explaining it all to the other archers.

"I'm not so good a rider," Bjorn said, "but I can try it."

Each of the archers took a horse and mounted it; each hauled a warrior up behind him. Muirtagh leapt onto the mare's back, strung the bow, and held down one hand to Bjorn. Bjorn swung himself up behind. Muirtagh reined the mare around and galloped straight for the right end of the line.

The others followed him. While they rode the fighting broke out again, the noise swelling up to frighten the crows and kites away. The closer they came the clearer the noise was, until Muirtagh could hear individual screams and groans, the gasps of effort. The mare ran in great frightened bounds, her ears pinned back, and the clash and ring of weapons seemed to seethe out of the earth beneath them.

A whole horde of Irish charged forward to meet them, their mouths gaping and their swords and spears like teeth. Muirtagh shot, dropping his reins and letting the mare pick her own way. Bjorn, one hand around Muirtagh's belt, leaned down to smash the Irish, and he shouted, "It's me, Bjorn, grown four more legs—start running, fools, it's Bjorn."

The mare jumped a fallen man and charged on. Muirtagh felt a brief tug at his belt, and the weight behind him slid off. Looking over his left shoulder, he saw Bjorn laying around him in the midst of the Irishmen, and the Irish scattered, giving him room, acknowledging him.

The mare thundered into the wood and Muirtagh dove off into a tangle of wind-drifted brush. He crawled away into the trees, while the mare bucked and neighed and plunged around inside the wood.

The others of the Danish archers poured in after him. Immediately, the hidden Irish attacked them, hauling them from their horses. Muirtagh knelt, lifted his bow, and shot whenever he could find a target through the trees; he heard one man howl.

"Over there," an Irish voice cried.

Muirtagh scrambled off through the brush. Thorns tore at him. He squirmed under an overhanging shrub, looked back, and saw them beating at the heavy bushes with their lances. He saw a big oak tree not far off and on hands and knees fought his way through the choking brush toward it.

The Danish had disappeared. He crouched with his back to the oak tree and watched for Irish. He caught a glimpse of red shirt and his hands jerked, but before he could lift the bow the man yelped and whirled into full view, an arrow thrusting from his hip. The Danes were still fighting.

The Irish dropped flat into the brush. Muirtagh arranged a dozen arrows around him and started shooting at whatever came close. He heard noises in the brush and shot, hoping they were not Danes.

A lance flashed out of the shrubs to his left and thudded into the oak, pinning him by the shirt and a bit of skin. He tore free, snatched up his arrows, and darted around behind the tree. He pressed his hand to his side. It hardly hurt, but he could feel his blood leaking down.

There was a low branch on this side. He slung the bow over his back, thrust the arrows into his belt, and jumped. He swung helpless a moment before he got up the strength to haul himself onto the branch.

The ivy had grown up the oak and in the lower branches screened him from below. He crouched, making himself small. He could see the Irish plainly now. Many of them were creeping along to encircle him; the others were lying still, their heads turning. They were searching each clump of brush with their eyes, looking for him.

Muirtagh shot carefully at the men in the back of the creeping group, so it was only when he missed the third shot a little and the man cried out that the Irish realized they were being fired at. They dodged into the bushes again, and Muirtagh scrambled up a few branches. Now he could see the Danes—they were in pairs, something he would never have thought of. They were crawling on hands and knees toward the Irish lying still. They had dropped their bows and taken up their daggers. Muirtagh shot at the prone Irish to keep them watching in the wrong direction.

Screaming war cries, the Danes attacked. The Irish whirled up to meet them. Muirtagh slid down the oak a little, looking for the other Irish.

Another lance rattled toward him, but the branches deflected it. Muirtagh could see none of them clearly enough to shoot. He shrank back against the tree, looking frantically all around.

A roar went up from the battlefield, and, jerking around, he saw Danes pouring into this wood. He climbed higher so that he could see the field. Through the branches he glimpsed Brodir's men charging after the Irish, and the Irish retreating wildly away from the wood, back toward their own center. The Irish below Muirtagh fled away through the trees, and the Danes, yelling like hounds, pursued them. One passed almost directly beneath Muirtagh, his sword waving over his head; the sword smacked into the oak's lowest branch, caught, and threw the man to the ground.

Muirtagh jumped down from the oak. The other archers were sitting on their heels, resting. Muirtagh said, "Find a good tree—the Irish will be calling a truce in a little while, to get their wounded in."

The archers nodded and obediently sought out trees. Muirtagh stood still, watching them. The wood was almost empty: the other Danes had run back to join their army. The sound of fighting was distant. He stood, re-laxed, not thinking.

Abruptly he hauled himself up. This was stupid. He turned to the oak and climbed into it again. He climbed high, up above the tops of the other trees around him, until he was even with the kites, and he saw that the whole of the Irish line was swaying back, staggering. He nocked an arrow and shot, and the arrow flew soaring over the trees into the heart of the Irish army. He doubted it had hit anything, and he laid the bow across his knees.

The Irish called for a truce, and the two armies stepped apart. Alone, wrapped around the branches of the oak, he watched them cart off their dead. The birds settled down to sip the blood on the ground. A few horses were grazing loose, behind the Danish camp, the chestnut mare among them.

He thought of Bjorn, springing into the midst of Irish, and how the Irish had given him room from the sheer terror of his name. Somewhere in there Eoghan stood, or lay already dead. Eoghan might tremble at the thought of meeting Bjorn Wolfbrother. Sometime he would have to tell Bjorn the end of Cuchulain's tale—how Cuchu-lain's enemies hadn't dared come near him, until a crow settled on his shoulder and gave proof that he was dead. In his mind he heard the low, measured strokes of the music, terrible and ravaged.

A horn blew.

It would be pleasant to be dead, to have it all done with. He felt how false that was. Like harp music, each note fighting, all these lives and hands moved vastly to-gether. Above the field, apart from it, he could feel some-thing of it—the fighting was picking up now, slower to get started than before. Like a dance, it arranged itself on the field.

There were men below him, in the wood, fighting. He heard their voices rising up to him like flames. He climbed down as fast as he could. A harsh Danish voice broke in the middle and somebody laughed, gasping. The branches obscured his view—he saw hands, long hair tossing, the glint of a blade. When he was close enough to see them clearly, all but one, a Dane, lay dead or badly hurt. The Dane had a gash in the leg, and the blood bolted out between his fingers. He sat down heavily beside a corpse, and even over the howling from the field Muirtagh could hear his heavy breathing.

Muirtagh leapt down and bent by the Dane. "Are you all right?"

"Give me—the chance to rest."

The man's face was slimy with sweat. Muirtagh trotted to the edge of the wood and knelt. He was within a few strides of the Irish. For a little while he had good shots, but the Danes were pushing the Irish back here and before long he had to climb a tree again.

A great shout rose up and he almost fell out of the tree, turning. Half the Danish line and all the Leinstermen were running backwards, before the wild charge of the Dal Cais. In the front of the Irish line the man in the gold raced, his head turned to shout to his men. Muirtagh shot at him and missed. They swung their shields up and thrust on, ignoring his arrows.

On the edge of the retreat already the men were turning their backs to the fighting. Along the forward line sparks and blood flew together, and the crows settled, their wings lifted high. The rest of the Danes were shifting madly, running sideways to keep contact with the retreating men, and the Irish, shrieking, bolted around to

encircle them. Muirtagh started to shoot, evenly, me-
thodically, into the backs of the Irish. He was almost out
of arrows, and he had no chance to get more.

Maelmordha like a great bird swung his horse and galloped down to his men. On the edge of the wood the
Danes were outflanking the Irish at last, but the Leinstermen, running, drew the Irish after them, and the Danes
too suddenly broke and fled. Muirtagh screamed out,
wordless. He looked toward the Leinstermen. They
were throwing down their swords and shields and running, and their voices rose in despair. Among them,
Maelmordha's great grey stallion galloped riderless.

The battle was entirely gone. Everywhere one man
fought one other, while half the Irish chased the Leinstermen. The Danes were struggling toward their ships,
keeping their faces toward the Irish, trying to hold them
off.

Muirtagh slid down out of the tree. Already men were
fighting in the trees. He heard shouting all around him—
Brodir's voice—"Come with me, come along, this is
over!"—Einar shouting pagan curses. Three men, Danes,
rushed panting through the wood.

Muirtagh raced toward the camp, hoping to catch a
horse. Some of the Irish were even stopping to loot bodies; they ignored him. Clear across the field he saw a knot
of Danes, the Jarl among them, encircled by Irish. He
swerved toward them, uncertain, and in a mad rush the
Irish swept over the Jarl and his men.

Einar was standing near the far edge of the wood, two
of his men at his back, fighting off a yapping band of
Irish. The Irish would move back, gather up, and fling
themselves at Einar, trying to carry him off his feet—it
was as if the two men with him were of no consequence.
Muirtagh nocked an arrow and ran up closer.

"Einar," Bjorn shouted. He was running up the field,

his hair and cloak wild, blood smeared over his face. He hurled himself into the Irish, one man into twenty. They whirled to meet him. Muirtagh went down on one knee and shot all but his last three arrows into the tangle, trying to keep from hitting Bjorn. The Irish wheeled and ran away, and Bjorn and Einar started up the field, toward Dublin.

Muirtagh raced to meet them. He'd done no running, and they were tired. He met them at the narrow meadow between the wood and the shore, with the Irish flying after them barking hoarsely, and Bjorn and Einar swung around to stand them off again. The Irish saw Muirtagh coming, whirled, and raced out of range. Muirtagh was so surprised he ran into Bjorn.

Bjorn and Einar got him by either arm and trotted off, hoisting him between them. "Let me down, I can run as well as you," he cried.

They stopped to catch their breath. Einar said, "I thought I was done, there. Why were you trotting around, like somebody's loose dog?"

Bjorn laughed. "They will not face me."

They ran on toward Dublin. The sun lowered and the clouds turned color. The Irish, mounted, were hunting them. Muirtagh heard a dog bay and his blood stopped in his heart.

A little way from the field, they came on Thorstein Hallson, sitting under a tree tying his shoelace.

"Come along," Bjorn said. His chest heaved deeply.

"No," Thorstein said. "The tide's at the flood, they can't get the ships out of the hop, and you'll have trouble in the river. Where am I to run to?"

Muirtagh nodded. "That's a wise man speaking."

Bjorn looked at Einar. "Must you be carried? Come along, child."

They ran on. Behind them, the dogs bayed closer. The

dark settled around them and Muirtagh stopped.

"No," he said. "I won't go farther. You hear the dogs. They'd catch you before the stars came out. I'll hold them, you go on."

"They'll kill you," Bjorn said.

"So. They'd kill you, too. Go on; have you lived so long to be brought down by dogs?"

Bjorn looked hard at him. "Well, then."

"God go with you."

"You pious little—" Bjorn caught Einar's sleeve and ran.

Muirtagh knelt in the high grass, nocked an arrow, and waited. Soon enough the horsemen with their leashed dogs appeared on the trail, moving at a brisk trot.

He drew back the bowstring and let the arrow fly. A dog took it through the chest, yelped, and died, tumbling his partner in the coupled leash head over heels. Muirtagh lay still in the grass. The Irish spread out, leaping off their horses.

"Who is it?" one shouted.

"Oh, guess at it," somebody else called. "Keep low, it's too dark for him to see much—"

Muirtagh shot at the voice and heard a howl of anger. "So much for you, Cormac ó Daugherty."

He had one arrow left, and he immediately regretted the long shot. He listened for them. They crept through the grass, hunched over, and he moved quietly toward Cormac. One of them thought to let a dog loose.

The dog snuffled and yelled, his belling hollow in the dark. Muirtagh thrust his bow into the back of his shirt and on hands and knees headed for Cormac. The dog sniffed him and galloped toward him. Muirtagh whirled, snatched out the bow, and shot the dog in mid-leap. The dog fell limply across Muirtagh's legs.

"Eoghan. Where's Eoghan?" Cormac shouted.

"Here," Eoghan said, way off to Muirtagh's left. His voice was steady, even mild. Muirtagh crept toward Cormac.

"Go in after him," Cormac said.

"Don't give orders to me."

"He'll not kill you."

Muirtagh was so close to Cormac he could hear the rustle of his clothes. He slithered around, unstrung his bow, and, leaping, slipped the string over Cormac's head. He flipped the bow itself in a circle. Cormac gasped, clutching at his throat, and Muirtagh jerked hard. Cormac went limp. Muirtagh dropped the bow and scrambled off.

A massive weight smashed into him, drove him down, and parched his face with its hot breath. He'd forgotten the other dog; it had not bayed. He whirled and drove his fingers frantically into the dog's dewlaps, keeping the slavering jaws from his throat. The dog's claws scratched him, tore his leg from hip to knee, and the dog with a twist of his head caught Muirtagh's forearm between his teeth. Muirtagh let go with the other hand and snatched out his dagger. The dog's slavering and snarls drove the sweat out of his body, and he heard himself sobbing. He thrust the dagger to the hilt in the dog's side, and the dog snarled into Muirtagh's face and snapped. His teeth grazed Muirtagh's cheek. One fang caught his lip. The dog whined and went limp.

But the men were standing over him, and when he threw the dog off the tip of a lance rested on Muirtagh's chest. "Stand up," the man at the other end of the lance said, in a cold voice. Muirtagh didn't recognize him.

Somebody lit a torch. The light spread over them, over their tight faces, set like masks. The man with the lance pulled a napkin out of his shirt and tossed it down. Muirtagh dabbed at his bloody face with it.

"Get Cormac's horse for him," Eoghan said. "Cormac will be needing it no more."

"I say kill him," the man with the lance said.

Eoghan's voice came quietly out of the dark. "Who is the chief here? He is my captive. We'll take him back. He is to be judged."

The circle of Irish broke up. They fetched in the horses and mounted. They bound up Muirtagh's arm and lashed his hands behind his back and his feet beneath the horse's belly. Eoghan rode over to pick up the reins; he carried Cormac's body in front of him on the black pony. Two other men rode up on either side of Muirtagh, and they started off toward the Irish camp.

"Did you get what I sent you, in Dublin?" Eoghan said.

"Yes."

Muirtagh shut his eyes. His face hurt, and he was exhausted. The same odd pride for Eoghan worked its way up through his body and he nodded his head.

"God's will be done," Eoghan said.

"The High King did you some honor, back at the beginning of the fight."

"I did the High King some honor," Eoghan said quietly.

"That was him, in the trees," the other man said—the man with the lance. "Who shot us down like deer."

"Why," Eoghan said, "who else could it have been?"

"You're arrogant, Eoghan."

Eoghan laughed. "Go lick your wounds somewhere else."

Muirtagh flexed his back, trying to ease out the ache. That might have been Aed's voice, come out of Eoghan's mouth. Aed's voice, the long yellow hair, the face Aed's and Cearbhall's—so. He remembered being in the tree and feeling the great quiet dancing. The blood had leapt the abyss.

"You're much changed, Eoghan," he said.

Eoghan stared down the men around him, so that they would pretend not to hear, and said in the steady voice, "Oh, things . . . happen. What wouldn't change you might easily change . . . a softer man, maybe. Things you'd not notice. I don't know. My mother—"

"Is she well?"

"Yes. She said I was to bring you home, if I could."

"I'm not going."

Into Eoghan's torchlit eyes something younger swam. "It shouldn't be so—what could you have done? It's over, finished, why can't you—"

"Be quiet. You are The ó Cullinane. When a chief asks a common man a question he asks it as a chief."

Eoghan flinched. He jerked the pony to a stop. "You. Fionn. Bring my captive back and see that he's treated properly." He whipped the pony away and galloped off.

They came at last to the tents. Fionn, the man with the lance, dismounted and cut Muirtagh's feet loose, and led him into the captives' tent. He tied one of Muirtagh's wrists to a stake and fetched him water and some bread.

"They'll have something of you for ó Daugherty's killing," Fionn said, and spat.

"The wounds of an animal are as those of a man, it says in the law. Now, get off. I was taken in a war and they'll have no penalties against me."

Fionn blushed red. "A man such as you—"

"You should pray God you'll never be a man such as me. Now, go."

Fionn stamped out. Muirtagh lay back, his wrist dangling awkwardly from the stake, and slept.

* * *

All the next day he lay in the tent, talking to Thorstein and two or three other captives. Thorstein was stretched out full-length on the ground; one of the King's sons had captured him and given him captive's peace because Thorstein had been sitting so calmly, waiting to be taken.

"So they got you, too, harper," he said, and yawned. "They killed Brodir, but not before Brodir had killed the King in his tent."

"Have you heard anything of Bjorn?"

"No. Eirik?"

Eirik rolled over, stretching. "Well, they caught me at the edge of Dublin, you know, and I saw two ships rowing out of the bay—one was Bjorn's, and I think maybe the other was Einar's. Sygtrygg's ship was gone, too."

"You ran with Bjorn, harper. How did you get captured and not him?"

"I got a crick in my side and sat down to rest, and they sent their dogs after me."

"Hnnh," Thorstein said. "We're not close enough to fight, so I'll call you a liar."

"How could I leave the holy land of Ireland?"

"You're an outlaw in the holy land of Ireland. That's reason enough."

"There are laws and laws."

Three Munstermen came in, knelt by Eirik, and cut him loose. Eirik sat up, rubbing his wrist. "You found it, then."

The shortest of the three grinned. "Under the front step, as you said. Now, get out of here before we decide it isn't enough."

"Are there any ships left in the river?"

"Well, it doesn't look as if we'll be able to take the fort at Dublin; we can't hold the harbor without it, and somebody said if you're on the shore Easter Sunday you might find a way home."

"Oh, well."

One of the other Munstermen said, "Thorstein, the King's son will give you your freedom tomorrow, if you give him your bond not to come to Ireland again."

"He has it, by your voice if that's enough, by mine too, if he comes to ask it."

The man turned to another captive. "They've gone to hunt for your gold, and if it's where you say it is, you're as free as Eirik."

"It's there—would I lie myself into a grave?"

The three Munstermen turned to Muirtagh.

"I knew we'd come to me, by and by," Muirtagh said.

"The ó Cullinane has given over your bond to the King. He says he'll stand neither for you nor against you, and he's gone back to his people already."

"Which King?"

The Munsterman laughed harshly. "Maelsechlainn, of course."

Going out the door, he paused. "They'll bring you up before him tomorrow. Pray, outlaw."

That evening they brought in water for the captives to wash in. Thorstein and the others made Muirtagh take the first turn at it—"You're battered up worse than we are, anyway," Thorstein said.

"You'll be washing in bloody water."

"I've done so before."

Muirtagh washed himself, cleaning out the wound in his leg, which he thought might fester. The dog's bite had been oozing all day. Between him and Thorstein, they got the arm unbandaged, cleaned, and wrapped up again.

"Why do we do all this for an arm that tomorrow night will be holding up the grass?" Muirtagh said.

"You should go tidy to your execution."

Muirtagh sat back, and Thorstein washed himself. "If we had a dagger, we could do something about your beard. It won't go any better for you if they think you've gone wild."

"Oh, they'll know me."

They talked all through the night—Thorstein told Muirtagh of the burning of Njal and his kin.

"If you see Bjorn, tell him—"

"I will. He'll come back—avenge you."

Muirtagh laughed, tried to stop, and laughed helplessly, until his eyes ran tears. "Oh, no, not that. No. Tell him I believe him, about the island he found."

"Frankly, I don't. He's a terrible liar."

"Tell him that to his face."

Thorstein grinned. "No, thank you."

They dozed in the first of the dawn. Muirtagh did not dream, and when they woke him up in the morning he felt as if the night had passed all in one moment.

"Did you sleep well, outlaw?"

"Never have I slept better."

They cut him loose, and he rose. To Thorstein he said, "Remember to tell that to Bjorn."

"What a mess of things you are," Thorstein said. "Ireland's losing a good harper."

Muirtagh shrugged. He let the guards tie his hands in front of him. They dropped a noose over his head, like a dog's leash, and led him out into the bright sunlight and across the field to Maelsechlainn's judgment place.

Maelsechlainn, for want of a stockade, was holding court in a makeshift earthworks. The remnants of the King of Ireland's army and Maelsechlainn's own, unblooded, stood like a stronger wall around the inside of the circle, and the chiefs and Kings sat around within that. Maelsechlainn was at their head.

"Now," Maelsechlainn said. "Here is a strange thing."

Muirtagh, aware of the bloodstains on his clothes, looked all around, at each of the chiefs and Kings. None of them would meet his eyes. He turned back to Maelsechlainn.

"You see how it is," Maelsechlainn said.

"How many pleasant faces you have about you, King."

Maelsechlainn sat back, his arms over the wide-spaced arms of his chair. He looked around, while the silence grew and spread. Slowly he lifted one hand and twined his fingers in his long white beard, and his small mouth pursed.

"Is there any man here who will speak for Muirtagh Aed's son of the ó Cullinane clan?"

Like dolmen stones, they sat, looking straight ahead, and Muirtagh could see their nervousness strain them.

"Not of the ó Cullinane," Maelsechlainn said in his King-voice. "It seems you disinherited yourself too early, Muirtagh."

Again the small mouth pursed, pink in the midst of the white beard.

"Not so," Muirtagh said. "It's only that I'll be dying rather late."

"Have you any excuse for what you've done—fought against your own people under rebels and Danes?"

"None that you do not know of already. Come to it, Maelsechlainn; judge me. It's for your saying, if you cast it off on someone else, then step out from under your crown."

Now the crowd murmured, at last, and they stirred unwillingly out of their containment. Muirtagh glanced at them and looked back at Maelsechlainn.

"I will say it," Maelsechlainn said. "There was another case we heard of here, and this must follow, I think. There is a certain justice in it the mind turns on. Who can trouble you more than you're troubled now? Go on. You are free."

His mouth twisted a little, saying it, as if it were sour on his tongue, and he looked over the heads of the men in their rings around him. "Let him free."

"Let it be so, then," Muirtagh said. A guard stepped forward and cut him free. Maelsechlainn stared into space; the other lords looked straight ahead, still once more. Muirtagh nodded. "I consent to it."

"Go away," Maelsechlainn said. "You are nameless, you are nobody."

"Why should I need a name? I'll harp myself into your blood and bones, King. What good's a name to me, when I'll have yours, and his, and every man in Ireland's?"

He walked to the way out of the earthworks, laughing under his breath. A guard was there, with his bow and a case of arrows. He dropped them at Muirtagh's feet and stepped away. Muirtagh grinned, bent down, and picked them up.

They were still all silent, back there. He turned and said, "You'll hear from me again, gentlemen, but you'll have to wait a bit. I left my harp in Dublin, and I must go get it."

He hung the arrow case from his belt and laid the bow across his shoulders. Whistling, he started down the road to Dublin to get his harp. Already, he could hear the music taking shape in his mind.

Cecelia Holland

Cecelia Holland was born in Nevada on New Year's Eve, 1943. Raised in Metuchen, New Jersey, she now lives in Woodbridge, Connecticut. She is the author of two earlier novels, *The Firedrake* (1966), dealing with the Norman invasion of England, and *Rakóssy* (1967), a novel of the Turk-Magyar wars of the early sixteenth century.